To Dave

Celestial Ambulance

With best wishes

Ann Matkins

Celestial Ambulance

Life – and work! – after death

Ann Matkins

Ann Matkins © **2012**

A record of this publication is available from the British Library.

ISBN 978-1-907203-45-9

Typesetting by Wordzworth Ltd
www.wordzworth.com

Cover design by Titanium Design Ltd
www.titaniumdesign.co.uk

Printed by Lightning Source UK
www.lightningsource.com

Cover images by Nigel Peace

Published by Local Legend
www.local-legend.co.uk

Dedicated to Keith, Andrew and Pamela.

Acknowledgements

My thanks to all my friends who have tolerated my need to get away sometimes and bury myself in words.

About the author

Ann Matkins spent the first thirty or so years of her life in London and Kent. Then with her husband and two children she emigrated to Melbourne, Australia, seeking a new and more spiritual life. Twenty years later she returned to England to put down new roots in rural Somerset.

Writing has been an abiding interest - travel journals, poetry and fantasy novels. Her hobbies include gardening and anything and everything to do with books and writing.

She has also published a collection of spiritual channellings:

How Love Works (Authorhouse UK Ltd, 2009)
ISBN: 978-1-4389-6103-3

About this book

This book began as a memorial to a dear friend.

One day I'd heard his voice say over the telephone, "I've got a year at the most, maybe less."

It was a shock – a shock that I had to share, which I did by meeting a mutual friend for coffee in a local café. It was while we shared our feelings of what was happening for Keith that the idea for the story first showed itself. Then the title appeared.

As soon as I got home I began typing the first chapter. My characters formed themselves in a neat row and made it very plain what it was they wanted me to say about them.

Keith didn't even have a year. He decided early on that he didn't want chemotherapy or any life-prolonging drugs. Six months later he was gone, very quickly. He'd been happy to relinquish his body from this life, knowing that there was more to look forward to.

The last I heard he was improving his education.

Contents

Contents

CHAPTER 1

The Big Question

"What do you think happens when you die, Ben?"

"Go to Heaven if I'm lucky."

"And will it be everything you hope for, or will it be one big surprise?"

Ben thought for a moment, anxious now about what sort of surprises might be in store for him. "Not too many surprises I hope."

"We shall see..." said the voice.

CHAPTER 2

The Operation

Ben knew all about hospitals. In his line of work it had been unavoidable, but he had never been on the receiving end before. He had served twenty-five years in the ambulance service before taking early retirement with a good financial package, and he had money saved too. A sweet life lay ahead of him with plenty of time still to enjoy it – or so he had thought.

Where had that time gone now?

Staring up at the ceiling of the oncology ward, he sighed in the manner of someone who believes that somewhere along the way he had pulled the short straw. Were the others in the ward faring any better? He looked around and counted the beds: four. One had curtains drawn across, a late arrival the evening before, nurses coming and going most of the night and also this morning. But nothing had been said. You could be in the next bed to someone and not know why they were in here.

He shifted his weight and pulled up the pillows. He had slipped down the bed again and his neck ached. The man in the next bed opened his eyes briefly, murmured softly and then closed them again. *Not likely to get anything out of him in the next few hours.*

Sister came bustling up ahead of the consultant. Curtains were swished around and suddenly Ben was cocooned against the outside world. It was a peculiar feeling, as if all communication, all connection with everything beyond the draped material, had suddenly ceased to exist. For now his world consisted of a bed, a bedside cabinet and a trolley for pills, a jug of water and a glass, face wipes and space for his meals. He didn't like hospital food - well no-one in their right mind would. There were choices, but the menu lied; in the end you got whatever was available. *Hospitals! Funny places,* he thought to himself. *We come here to get better or to die. Poles apart, those two events, and yet somehow the body has to rest in order to decide which way to go. Either way, whatever happens we exit through the same doors.*

The two almost-strangers stood either side of his bed. Up until then they had been on the periphery of his life, but now they were his lifeline. He squirmed uncomfortably with his thoughts, feeling out of control with events. He'd always been self-reliant. Well, perhaps that wasn't exactly true. He had a partner, and together they relied on each other. *She would be relying on him now to get better! Hold that thought.* Was *he going to get better? And why was he fretting about something that hadn't even happened yet?* As he gazed at these two people he hardly knew, he wished with all his might that somehow their professional expertise would make all the difference to the outcome. For suddenly he realised he couldn't change anything about it himself.

He hoped the consultant didn't notice his mood. He didn't.

"The tumour is operable." This was said in a brisk voice, straight-faced, but encouraging.

"That's good, then," Ben had replied, on the verge of enthusiasm, but not quite sure how enthusiastic he really felt. And there was that feeling again of having no control over events, or whether others had any more control than he did.

The consultant had little more to say, except that Ben would be booked in for the operation as soon as possible. "Meanwhile, go home. Be with your family."

Ben didn't have family, except for his partner, Linda - his parents having passed away many years before; he and Linda had never had children. But the consultant didn't know that.

Up until a few weeks ago, Ben had thought of himself as a fairly fit and healthy fifty-eight-year old; good for another twenty or at least ten years, except for his lack of energy. Linda had insisted he go to the doctor's for a blood test; he tried to shrug the matter off, thinking the tiredness would pass, but Linda persisted. The results had come back more quickly than expected.

Linda was still at work when Ben had arrived home after seeing the doctor for the second time. He had immediately switched on the kettle and reached for the tea caddy. His hands fumbled as he pulled off the tin lid, and he was suddenly cross with himself for his clumsiness. Several cups of tea later, Linda found him slumped in the kitchen chair, elbows on the table, head in his hands.

"You can tell me," was all she said.

"It's funny," he murmured, his shoulders shaking. "I don't feel a thing."

"Ben." Linda knelt by the chair, wrapping her arms around him, head pressed into his shoulder. "Are you laughing or crying?"

"I'm doing both," he sighed, sitting back and looking down at her with sparkling eyes. "I just think it must be a great joke because I don't feel any pain, or even feel ill. I mean all I wanted was not to feel so tired. That's all, just not so tired. And now this! But the doctor was quite definite about the cancer."

"Oh, Ben," Linda choked back a tear. "I'm so sorry."

"Don't be, luv. I'm ok with it."

It had been a month since the first diagnosis. Now, as he waited by his hospital bed for Linda to come and take him home, Ben wondered how he could go back to living a normal life for the next few days and not think about the operation to come. He just couldn't imagine how he'd do it.

Linda saw his mood as soon as she walked into the ward; with a determined look on her face that Ben recognised, she said, "Ok, my man, I'm taking us out for lunch. None of your 'straight home' nonsense!"

They had lunch at the Bridge Inn by the river: steak, chips and salad. Well, Linda ate her salad and Ben didn't touch his. "Can't see the point," he always said when she'd determinedly served up salad at least once, if not twice, a week. She would *hmmph* and tell him it was good for him and he needed his vitamins – but he still wouldn't eat it.

They sat outside in comfortable silence for a while, watching the ducks on the river, each in their own thoughts. Ben tried to rivet his on the beautiful sunny day and the comfort of having Linda to enjoy it with.

"We don't do this often enough," she sighed.

He smiled at her, sensing that she was probably already planning more things they didn't do enough of; her way of taking his mind away from what was to come, and maybe it would help her too. "The consultant said he was going to book me in for the operation as soon as possible."

"Yes, I know," she replied. "I saw him too. That's good then, isn't it?" She looked hopeful. "Eat up your salad. You need your strength."

Ben just grinned at her and left the salad.

Within a week he was back in the oncology ward and scheduled for theatre at ten o'clock the next morning. In the end it was all happening in a rush.

"Not a minute to lose," had been the final words of the consultant, accompanied by a warm but slightly crooked smile. It was meant to be encouraging. It wasn't.

The ward doors swung open; a trolley, a ward orderly and Sister arrived at his bedside, with a bit of chat from the orderly, keeping things light. Ben smiled. He knew the ropes.

As the trolley wound its way to the operating theatre his mind flickered to scenes of others who'd been wheeled down this corridor before him, knowing now how they might have felt. Sister smiled down at him.

I'm being well looked after. Just relax. It will all be all right!

In the prep room the anaesthetist stood on one side, his assistant on the other. Ben couldn't help thinking they both looked far too young. The assistant made small talk – more clever distraction while the anaesthetist prepared the patient. After the first few words, Ben's world became as if it had never been, as he quietly slipped into unconsciousness.

Oblivion.

The operation went well. But the patient died.

CHAPTER 3

Waking Up

Ben opened his eyes a fraction. His body felt strange: not so weak, a good sign, he thought. Tiredness wrapped around him like a warm blanket and he drifted back into a light slumber.

There was a feather-like touch on his shoulder.

"I'm not ready to wake up yet," he said, enjoying another moment of perfect rest such as he had never felt in all his life before. *Must be the morphine.*

The gentle hand would not go away.

He opened his eyes wide this time; someone gazed down at him, deep violet eyes tilting into a smile.

"Who are you?" he asked, somewhat surprised. Although she looked very much like a nurse, she was not one Ben could remember and he had a good memory for faces. He looked around for Sister. She was nowhere to be seen. And another thing he noticed - the ward looked different. He was sure it had been a four-bedded one, but now he seemed to have a room all to himself. *Way to go!* he thought to himself with a slight smugness that didn't quite manage to forget the well-being of others. But the walls seemed less solid than they should have been, a bit too hazy and veil-like, and through them he could see movement, people. A glance around the room made him appreciate its spaciousness, a lingering scent of roses and violets, and sunshine pouring in through the French windows. *And that sky! God, it looks so blue!* He gazed at the nurse again. No, he still didn't recognise her.

She saw his puzzled expression and said reassuringly, "I'm here to help you to where you are needed."

Needed? Ben sank back on his pillows and couldn't think where he'd be needed - not right now, not having just gone through major surgery for cancer. Perhaps time had slipped by more quickly than he'd realised. Could his memory be that bad? He knew an anaesthetic could do funny things to the brain. He looked more carefully at the nurse standing by his bed, noticing for the first time her crisp, starched uniform, her hair covered by a white veil, wisps of honey curls trying to escape. He couldn't remember when he'd seen a uniform so smart and crisp, and it looked... well... oddly old-fashioned. She smiled at him again with those wonderful violet eyes. He closed his, suddenly very tired and not caring what the nurse's uniform looked like, or anything else for that matter.

"Can you come back in a bit? I'm feeling rather knocked out."

"In a way, you are," came the smiling reply.

"How d'you mean?"

"Doesn't it all look different?"

It smelled different, too. He craned his neck to see if someone had brought in a vase of fresh flowers, and a small doubt began to form in the back of his mind. He remembered going to sleep and having a wonderful dream, a bright, warm light, loving arms... bliss... and then he'd woken up here.

"Have I been moved to a different hospital?"

"You could say that," said the nurse. "You're still not sure where you are, are you - or what has happened?"

"I know I've had an operation and I'm here, still alive."

"Alive, yes, but in what circumstances?"

Now it was the nurse asking the questions, and this puzzled Ben. He thought it should have been just him, seeing as he was the one in the bed. *Circumstances* she'd said - that seemed to be the key word; and then his brain began the slow process of putting two and two together. It took him a moment to think it through. *The operation!*

"I'm not dreaming am I? And I'm not back where I thought I would be. I've..." He could hardly say the words. It was all so final. "So that's it. I've died!"

"Yes, to your Earthly life it would appear so."

Ben dropped his head back on the pillow. "Well I'll be... It's a bit of a shock, nurse," he stammered. "I just never... Oh my God, it happens so quickly in the end, doesn't it? Who'd have thought..." But then he stopped, suddenly remembering those he'd left behind.

"Don't be sad, Ben. You will discover that not all loved ones get left behind. Just wait and see."

He couldn't imagine what she meant. *Not left behind? But they weren't ill! God, I hope they're all right.*

"It's ok," said the nurse. "They are all as well as when you left them."

Into his thoughts came his Linda. How was she finding life now that he was here and, well, not with her? She was a brave lady, he knew that. She had been always there for him, especially after the diagnosis.

The nurse smiled reassuringly. "They will miss you, that is to be expected, but visiting hours are not restricted here."

Ben couldn't work out what she meant. *Visiting hours? How did that work?*

"You will see," came the answer.

Everything seemed so extraordinary and different, and yet so ordinary too. Here he was in what felt like a conventional hospital bed, though that seemed to have suddenly, peculiarly, changed to a comfortable couch-like affair. He was a living breathing person, who, when he thought about it, felt more alive than he had in many years. He started to grin. Feeling so alive, that was great; but being in a place that he had only thought about in his imagination, that was something else. Was this for real?

"So I'm still alive and kicking?" He pinched himself just to make sure.

"It would appear so," said the nurse.

"And I'm better? Really well? I don't need more surgery?"

"No."

"How long do I have? I mean, how long before I'm an outpatient?"

"Don't be in such a hurry, Ben! You won't be discharged straight away. First of all we need to check out your legs. You'll still feel weak, but a short walk should do you more good than staying in bed all the time, and I think you're up to it."

Ben nodded. He was beginning to feel stronger by the minute; energy was pulsing through his muscles like a river in full flow, ready to burst its banks.

"I'll be back once you're dressed. Take your time."

There was a pair of jeans on the chair next to his bed and a very clean, very white shirt. Under the chair was a pair of white trainers - no socks. Feeling a sudden desire to get out of bed, he swung his legs over the side and stood up quickly, but it was too soon; his legs weren't keeping up with the rest of him, and he started to fall over sideways. A ward orderly passing by gave him a wink and was suddenly by his side.

"All right, mate?" the man said light-heartedly, supporting Ben around the waist. He sat him down on the bedside chair. "Having trouble staying upright?"

"Yes. Thanks," replied Ben, wondering how the man had managed to rush to his aid in less than a split second. "First day up. Bit wobbly." The orderly nodded as if in acknowledgement that everyone was the same the first day out of bed.

The nurse appeared just as he had finished buttoning up his shirt. She took hold of his hand and in no time at all they seemed to be somewhere else altogether, a lighter space. There had been no move-ment that he was aware of; one minute he was in the ward, the next where he was now. He glanced behind him, but the hospital had disap-peared and in front of him a wide expanse of green lawn stretched out to the far horizon. How did that all happen?

"That's lovely," he said, as a passing remark about the lawn.

"There's more," said the nurse.

He was glad. Lawns were great, even if they looked as if someone had mown them just five minutes ago, but there had to be more to the Other Side than this...

"Be patient. We're waiting for someone."

Ben found it difficult to be patient now that he'd got used to the fact of where he was. His mind raced ahead trying to think who might be coming to meet him. Maybe it was his Mum and Dad, though the nurse had said it was some*one*.

It wasn't his Mum, or his Dad, and he suddenly noticed the nurse had disappeared.

"Greetings," came a great booming voice. Ben looked up at a tall figure dressed in a dazzling white robe, edged with an amethyst band.

"Hello. Sorry, you are...?"

"Horace is as good a name as any."

Ben didn't think he looked much like a Horace, in fact definitely not like one, and said as politely as he could, "That's not your *real* name though, is it?"

The Great Wise Being smiled down at Ben, a twinkle in his eye. "You don't remember me, do you?"

"We've met before?"

"Yes, in your dreams, which you have a habit of not remembering."

"Oh, sorry."

"Perfectly normal. It is good to see you Ben."

Ben was in a bit of a daze, wondering why a stranger was welcoming him when his parents were nowhere to be seen. After all they *were* family.

"You will see them again," said Horace, picking up on Ben's thoughts. "You've probably forgotten they were here to meet you when you first arrived. You were rather 'out of it' at the time."

Ben realised then that he couldn't remember anything between having his pre-med at the hospital on Earth and waking up in what he now knew was officially called the Lodge of Rest and Recuperation (though most people referred to it as 'the hospital'). He shook his head, disappointed that he had no memory of seeing his parents; but he hadn't forgotten his manners and politely held out his hand. The handshake was returned with a warm, firm grip.

Horace, or whatever he chose to call himself, was an impressive man to behold, so tall that Ben felt he would get a crick in his neck if they were ever to have a long conversation standing up. Ben's hair was brown, but Horace's shoulder-length hair was as dark as a raven's wing, a sharp contrast to his almost luminous white skin. And Ben couldn't help noticing how very comfortable he looked in that loose white robe.

He looked down at his own jeans and white shirt. "Is this what I must wear from now on?" he asked.

"Not at all - you wear whatever you choose. We have a catalogue you can order from, just a thought away."

"I've not yet caught on to the 'thought' thing, but I guess it will come naturally."

"Oh yes. It doesn't take long."

The big man looked fondly at his young companion. "You are recovering well and should be discharged very soon. I think, therefore, it is time we talked about your future."

"The nurse mentioned I was needed somewhere, but I didn't quite understand what she meant by it."

"Contrary to universal belief, life does not come to a lazy full stop here, Ben. You will have a job to do."

"Really?" came the vague response that had no curiosity in it at all. His brain was still too busy with the concept of being where he was to think about anything as mundane as a job.

"At first, I expect it will be something you will feel able to handle easily. And of course you will have a chance to further your education."

"*Education?*" Ben wasn't sure he'd heard that correctly.

"Yes," Horace confirmed. "It's true. There are vast possibilities here that you can take advantage of."

"But I was never any good at it; and anyway what's all this about a job? Why do I need one? Doesn't anyone get time off for good behaviour in Heaven?"

"This is not Heaven, Ben."

"Bbbut…" spluttered Ben, suddenly confused. "So, where are we?"

"Some call this the Summerland. It's a very good description."

"So what happened to Heaven?"

"That is something to aspire to," was the patient reply. "It has to be earned. But where you are now is a very good place to begin attaining that goal, and that is why education is so important. As, of course, is being of service. There is much for you to take in just now, but what is to come we are sure will not disappoint." Horace was smiling, though to Ben the smile was a little bit too amused. "There is much to look forward to, Ben, and many places to visit. Don't worry, there will be plenty of leisure time before any of this needs to happen."

Ben felt somewhat relieved to hear there might be leisure time.

"You did have some education on Earth, did you not?" Horace continued.

"Oh, you mean school? Yes, well I did as much as I needed to, but promptly forgot most of it when I left."

"And after school?"

Ben scratched his head, trying to work out what Horace could be hinting at.

"Cast your mind back, Ben. You surely haven't forgotten everything."

Slowly, as if his brain had been hiding the information until this very moment, Ben became aware of one of the most meaningful - if rather short - chapters of his life.

"Do you... do you mean the philosophy group?"

"Aha, the boy remembers! Yes, Ben. And didn't they also teach you how to meditate?"

"Yes, that's right, but..."

"Hmm?"

"...I was only with the group for a couple of years and then I left; never meditated again. Lack of discipline I suppose, couldn't keep it up. It's an old trick of mine. My mind wanders to other things and life suddenly veers off in a different direction of its own accord... Or I allow it to," he added, a little sheepishly.

"You led a good, kindly life, Ben. There's nothing wrong in that. Don't discount your achievements."

Ben's mind could picture how it was back then, in his early twenties. The philosophy group had been run by a rather quiet, timorous Englishman married to a chatty and personable Scottish lady. There he had learned the value of finding the stillness within, opening up a universe of possibilities that allowed him to explore ideas normally beyond the reach of rational thought.

"They were good times," he sighed. "What a blimmin' shame I never kept it up."

"But by now, being where you are, you must have come to realise that what you saw and understood in your meditations - even though you thought it was all just your imagination - was, and is, in fact very real."

Ben grinned. "Yes, well, that's true enough. In fact it's a lot more beautiful, and a lot more real, but the *feeling* of it all is much the same as I imagined it. It's really like coming home, isn't it?"

"Yes, truly it is. So, for now, just draw into yourself the blessedness of this place, and know that if you need me I am just a thought away. I answer every call, no matter where I am. I'll see you again very soon."

And with that the Great Wise Being disappeared, melting into the ether and leaving Ben to admire the view on his own. The lawn had by now transformed itself into several tree-lined avenues, and the radiant colours of flower-filled gardens glowed in a sublime harmony that seemed to explode through his heart and out through his fingertips. As he stepped onto one of the paths he couldn't help but blow out his cheeks in wonder.

If this wasn't Heaven, then it was a bloody good imitation.

In no hurry to leave the gardens, Ben found a bench that stood beneath the feather-like branches of a weeping willow, and mused for a while about this new life and what might come next - which Horace had indicated would include a job and education! Things academic were not to be dwelt on so his thoughts drifted to his parents. He hadn't seen them yet – or rather been conscious enough to remember when they had visited. "But I'm ready for you now!" he said out loud. And a voice inside his head told him to be patient.

Patience! Probably need practice with that.

"Relax!" said a voice.

So Ben tried relaxing.

"*Relax!*"

"I'm trying."

"Let your mind drift."

Ben tried, allowing his eyes to half-close as he gazed into the distance. His body felt loose, almost numb. Slowly his vision blurred, became unfocused, and he began to feel the essence of where he was more intensely. A warmth crept through his body, a surge of peace. He gave into it and closed his eyes.

He woke with a start, suddenly aware that the world around him was different - the gardens had disappeared; he was back in his old home, in the kitchen. A woman stood by the sink, her back to him. She was humming a tune. He recognised it instantly, a favourite. Ben held the vision in his mind, instinct telling him not to let go of his focus. Lose the focus and he would lose the thread of being here.

The woman half-turned towards him, letting out a small sigh.

"I'm here, luv," he said, hardly daring to breathe. *Crazy man,* he thought. *She can't hear you!*

Linda turned back to peeling the potatoes and carrots that sat in a pan of cold water. Ben looked over her shoulder, catching her energy as she felt the ripple of his closeness: a slight shudder, nothing more.

He had to step back quickly as she turned and half-ran to the living room. The vegetable peeler hit the water in the pan with a soft splash - beyond her hearing, but clear as a peal of bells to his.

A towel grabbed in haste… wiping hands dry on the way… reaching up to a shelf… picking a special book. It fell open to the words of a poem:

> *Let the world see the light*
> *Of our souls' desire,*
> *That does not end*
> *With death.*
> *For love sustains all*
> *And never separates,*
> *Only brings everything together as one.*

Linda closed the book. "Hello, Ben," she said quietly to herself.

Ben gave her a hug before he left, or as close as he could get to giving her a hug. Light filled her aura and tears rolled down her cheeks, but they were tears of joy, not heartache.

"I'll come again, luv. I promise. I've got work to do, but when you need me, just call and I will hear you."

Linda nodded. Ben hoped she nodded because she had heard his words, if not directly by his voice, then maybe they had entered her mind. It didn't matter how she'd heard them.

A remembrance of his light kiss on her cheek came back with him. He opened his eyes and blinked to clear his vision. It had been an instant only, but in his heart he felt the link between Linda and himself was as strong as ever, and that was a blessing greater than anything. Emotions surged through him: joy, sadness, love, acceptance... The list went on.

He was still coming to terms with what had just happened when something bumped into his leg – rather hard. *What on Earth?*

Looking down he saw a rather scruffy little West Highland terrier looking up at him, tongue lolling out of the side of its mouth, ears pricked in expectation.

"Rufus, you old scallywag. You're here, you're actually *here*!"

This was the next best thing to being with Linda or seeing his parents. He picked up and hugged the much-loved and long-remembered friend from his childhood. Rufus's tail was wagging like a high-powered metronome. And Ben said a silent prayer of thanks to whoever had arranged this.

The little dog licked Ben's face all over as the special spot behind its ears was thoroughly paid attention to. And then something amazing happened - its fur began to get sleeker and whiter.

"Why Rufus, you're making magic!"

"And don't you think I look handsome? You may not have recognised me if I'd appeared looking as I am now."

"You can talk!"

"Not talk exactly," said Rufus. "You can understand everything I'm saying because we're on the same wavelength here. It's more like you're tuning into my mind."

"Well, it certainly works for me. And you're right, I wouldn't have recognised you as you are now. Clever, thoughtful dog!"

Ben had never given much consideration as to whether animals could inhabit the Summerland, or even whether humans could communicate in such a way with their pets, knowing their innermost thoughts as he was knowing the little dog's now. "Wow," he said out loud, "this sort of communication is truly fantastic."

"And there are other things you'll find out," said Rufus. "Other things you can do. You wait and see."

Ben stroked Rufus's head, feeling that sense of companionship that fills a gap, however small, and makes you believe that all is right in the world.

★

CHAPTER 4

Station One Two Zero

Full recovery was quick for Ben and he was soon ready to be discharged from the hospital. A nurse came to check he had everything he needed. She nodded with satisfaction at his smart new jeans and crisp, white shirt open at the neck.

"You'll do," she said with a bright smile on her face. "Nervous?"

"Just a little."

"Always the same, this next step, venturing forth into a new world. It will fit you like a glove, though. I've never heard anyone complain. Don't worry."

Ben looked down at his feet noticing not the trainers he had on before, but a brand new pair of sandals, brown leather, soft and supple. He wriggled his toes, feeling a freedom that surged through his body like a wellspring of hope and anticipation. Sliding his shoulders back and taking a deep breath, he checked again that he had what he needed, which was very little – just the clothes he stood in and a piece of paper with all his details. He wasn't sure where he was headed, but he knew he would find out before long.

He took one last look around his room, remembering how it had been when he had first arrived. Comfort and peace of mind for the patient was paramount, so he had only seen what would be familiar to him - wards looking just like those on Earth, conventional. Once he'd accepted where he was he'd experienced a transformation of his surroundings; his hospital bed suddenly becoming a comfortable couch contained in its own cubicle of light, a light that shone with brightness but that never hurt the eye. Through this light filtered the many coloured rays that altered and adapted to whatever healing the patient required. It seemed to him that anything was possible in the Lodge of Rest and Recuperation, including the ability to shapeshift its atoms and molecules according to the awareness, beliefs, and psychological comfort zones of any one of its inpatients.

Now, as Ben stood outside in the clear, bright air, knowing his healing was complete - even the Outpatients Department had said there was no need for him to come back and had signed him off – he wondered what to expect next.

One of the nurses had followed him out. "Are you Ben?"

"Uh-huh," he nodded.

"I'm to take you to the Market Place."

"Do I need to go to the Market Place?" he asked.

"Well, it's a good place to start. That's where you can find out what sort of work you'll be doing. You've got your bit of paper?"

"Um, yes," he replied nervously. "Oh, yes, of course."

Work! He remembered what Horace had told him, that the Summerland was a place where you could continue to lead a useful life. Suddenly there seemed all sorts of possibilities. But what were they?

Then a strange thing happened. One minute Ben was standing outside the hospital with the nurse and the next he was in the Market Place. The nurse was nowhere to be seen. Before him lay a large piazza, complete with a fountain in the middle, around which were placed brightly coloured awnings of green and white or blue and white canvas, covering what looked like conventional market stalls.

People milled all around, greeting him with smiles and coming up to shake his hand in welcome. Some were dressed in working clothes - dungarees, or casually elegant business suits, and some in loose, baggy clothing - these in all the colours of the rainbow as well as some colours he'd never seen before. Ben looked down at his own clothes and smiled, thinking how they could have easily come from his own Earthly wardrobe, and he wondered if jeans and a white shirt were standard issue when you first arrived. He made a mental note to check the catalogue. For the moment, though, the sincerity of his welcome made him feel more at home than he'd expected. The hubbub of activity around him was infectious, and he soon felt a growing desire to take on any work that might be cast his way. Then he began to wonder what sort of work might be available. What did people do in the Summerland that you could call *work*; and what, if he had the choice, would he want to do?

There were choices, curious choices for some. One tall, dark-haired lad, bare-shouldered and dressed in green dungarees, was carting away what looked like a sack of potatoes.

That's a bit odd, he thought. *Potatoes?*

"He's working on an improved gene," came a voice from behind.

Ben turned around and met the clear, grey eyes of someone who reminded him of an elf he'd once seen in a book when he was about seven years old. This elf had pointed ears that twitched non-stop, and a quirky mouth that kept changing from a cheeky grin to a rather unhappy scowl, and then back again. He wondered if this was merely a reflection of the elf's thoughts, or whether he actually had no control over his mouth. Or perhaps, even, this person was floating between two dimensions and hadn't quite mastered the art of staying wholly in one place before transferring to another and was therefore reacting to two different situations. Ben hoped the elf wasn't scowling because of him.

All these thoughts travelled through his mind at a tremendous rate, so it was only within the twinkling of an eye that he found himself saying without thinking, "Who are *you*?" in that rather peremptory way people have when taken by surprise. But then pulling himself up smartly he added, "I'm sorry. I don't believe we've been introduced."

"No need," was the laughing reply. "But in case you really have to know, I'm Hendrish."

"Pleased to meet you, Hendrish," replied Ben, still slightly taken aback by the appearance of the elf, who really was remarkably like a character who might exist in the imagination of someone who wrote fairy stories. "Um... I'm Ben," he said at last.

"Yes, I know. It's written all over you."

Ben looked nonplussed at this, and hastily felt all over his back in case there was a sign there saying: *This is Ben. He's the new-kid-on-the-block.*

"It's all right," said Hendrish in a voice that sounded high and thin, but not tinny. "I know who you are, the same as everyone knows who you are. It's not hard, you know."

"I haven't experienced the easy bit yet," complained Ben, but then he felt guilty that he should be complaining at all, considering where he was... He excused himself by saying, "I'm still finding my way around."

"Which is why you're here, in the Market Place."

"Well, I was told it was a good place to start."

"Sure is. Now, my dear," continued Hendrish, "you were curious about the potatoes."

"Yes, and from what you've said I gather they conduct experiments here. Is that in order to improve things for people back home?"

"You mean on Earth? Yes, that's right, all sorts of experiments. Perhaps you might like to think about a job in one of the laboratories? That's if you haven't made up your mind about what you want to do."

"Thanks, but if it's all the same I'd rather not be a laboratory technician. Never was very good at science, and hopeless at gardening. In fact I never tried it. Not even house plants."

"Oh well, that explains a lot," said Hendrish, who promptly disappeared, never to be seen again.

"Win some, lose some," Ben muttered under his breath.

He turned to see there were now queues of people lining up in front of the tented stalls. He watched to see what happened, wanting to make sure he knew what to do when it came to his turn. It seemed once you arrived at the head of a queue, you were handed a slip of paper; this was studied carefully, sometimes leading to a conversation with the person at the stall, fingers pointing to some detail that perhaps needed clarifying. Then, satisfied, people moved on. But it was very odd, they just sort of disappeared – one minute there, the next not. It took some getting used to, this strange new world.

As he was mulling over how anyone could appear and disappear at random, a resonant voice boomed out from behind. He turned to face a large, comfortably round figure dressed in a blue boiler suit and cap.

"Hello," Ben said tentatively to the stranger.

"Hello," came a gravelly reply. "You're new, aren't you?"

Ben sighed inwardly. How was he ever going to get rid of that new look? As if in answer the man said, "You've got that faraway expression on your face. Haven't quite got used to everything you're experiencing. By the way, my name's Tom. I help down at the depot, which is where you and I are expected. I'm to talk to you about what you may want to do next. I understand you're well recovered. You *are* ready to work aren't you?"

"Oh yes," said Ben, "more than ready."

"I also understand," said Tom, "that you used to be an ambulance man in your former life. Is that right?"

"Yes, that's right," agreed Ben, wondering where this conversation was leading.

"Well then, we shall see what's on offer for you."

Ben felt his whole body shimmering; it was not an unpleasant feeling – as if for a moment his body had forgotten where it was. He had experienced it once before, only then it was a case of leaving his physical body behind on an operating table.

In the space of a millisecond he was at Station One Two Zero, with Tom still by his side. The place was buzzing with activity.

"It's an ambulance station!" Ben gasped in disbelief. He hadn't expected this. *Why did they need ambulances?*

Tom could hear his thoughts. "They're very useful when it comes to rescuing people who need our help."

"Can't you just, well, suck people up into the astral?" No, maybe *suck up* was the wrong way to put it. "I mean, transfer them?"

"We're short of people who have your know-how. There are many who need our help. Don't worry, you'll pick everything up as you go along. Once an ambulance man, always an ambulance man, eh?"

Ben looked at Tom as if he was talking out of the back of his head. He couldn't believe what he was hearing. "I'll be driving an ambulance? You're saying this is my job from now on? But I did that for twenty-five years already. Isn't that enough?"

"But you see... we need your expertise."

Ben ran fingers through his hair, feeling more bemused than ever, while Tom smiled reassuringly at him. *It must be a bit different, seeing as I'm in a different dimension and all.* But he couldn't stop himself muttering under his breath some incoherent words that expressed something of what he was feeling, such as this was not what he had expected. Then out loud, he said, "Ok, I'll do it."

Tom raised an eyebrow as if to say, "Did you really think you had any say in the matter?"

In his quiet way, Ben had lived what he could only think of as an ordinary Earthly life. He had left his parents' home when he was in his early twenties, having already experienced a shaky start at various equally uninspiring jobs. After leaving school with the minimal amount of academic qualifications, he went into a large bank as a filing clerk, eventually proving his worth and becoming a counter assistant. His interest in handling other people's money soon palled, however, and he moved on, taking up a job as a clerk to a local divorce lawyer, where `phone calls came thick and fast. He organised clients' files (the secretary never had time) and became very efficient at tidying up correspondence, putting cases in their right order according to when the client had contacted them, rather than in order of his boss's preference; and he had made endless cups of tea and coffee not only for Mr Hunter but also for the secretary. His boss was the most disorganised person he had ever met and the secretary was extremely grateful for Ben's skills in that direction, always saying he made her life so much easier, and fluttering her eyelashes at him.

In the end, though, the idea of supporting someone in a business that survived on the fallout of people who could no longer tolerate living together began to take its toll, and he looked around for a more congenial situation. He eventually applied for a position as a porter in a nearby hospital and that was where he had met his Linda - a nurse on the oncology ward. When the time came for him to move into that ward, Linda had already been working at the retirement home for ten years. When she visited him, she remarked how strange it was to be coming back, not being one of the staff any longer; but some familiar faces were still there and Ben thought it had helped her to catch up with old friends – given her the support she needed and that he felt he wasn't quite able to.

It was while working at the hospital that he began to appreciate the skills of the ambulance men (he had never got used to calling them paramedics). That was a while ago now and the world had moved on, never tiring of re-inventing names and labels that suited the times we lived in. He had changed his job again and never regretted it. And here he was picking up where he'd left off. Well, almost.

Tom introduced Ben to Denis, the station superintendent, who looked Ben up and down with a critical eye, then smiled warmly and put out his hand. People were very polite here.

"Welcome, Ben," he said, shaking hands vigorously. "We are a bit short-staffed just now, so I'm really glad you've decided to come on board."

Ben reflected that really he couldn't remember having had much say in the matter, but now was not the time to bring that up. "Thank you, sir."

"No sirs here, my lad, call me Denis. You've met Tom, of course, and there's Steve and Brian and all the others, but you'll meet them all in time. Most are out on missions at the moment, except Steve. He's one of our hands-on men in the Maintenance Department."

"You have a Maintenance Department? And missions?"

"Oh yes, the ambulances need to be kept in mint condition of course, otherwise we wouldn't be able to do the rescues. 'Rescue work' is what we call our missions. Oh, I suppose you haven't had anyone explain to you yet exactly what goes on here. Well, there you go, maybe this was the best time to tell you anyway." And with that Denis took Ben into his office and sat him down and spent the next few minutes outlining what Ben's responsibilities would be, and how everything ran on well-oiled wheels, and that he was not to worry if he felt like a new boy because he was sure that having been an ambulance man once he would pick up everything in no time at all.

"So you run the station in much the same way as happens down on Earth? But there must be some differences, surely!" queried Ben.

"Well, the differences are that you are working in a different dimension and our technology is streets ahead of what you've experienced before, but then that's to be expected seeing as we operate in a different reality and Earthly physicality no longer exists to hinder us in any way."

Ben swallowed. His body still felt physical and solid, and his brain still worked as normal. It was weird. He clenched and unclenched his hands just to make sure that everything was in working order. Where he was now didn't feel so very different from the memory of his former life, except that he knew he had died, so therefore it *had to be different*; and he rationalised that what felt like the physical part of him was really another sort of body altogether, whose molecules were vibrating at a different rate, more ethereally. Or that's how he understood it. He gave his head a vigorous scratch to reassure himself he was still connected to something that felt halfway solid and real, though he had to admit that with every passing minute he felt more alive than he had in his entire previous life.

"So," said Denis, cutting across his thoughts, "are you ready to join the crew and rescue those who need our help?"

"Yes, I guess so. From what you've told me, being an ambulance man here is all about helping people who've died but are having a problem knowing what to do next. That's new stuff for me, but I guess you're also saying it won't seem that different once I get into the swing of things."

Denis nodded. "That's it, lad. Now, Tom, I think it's time you introduced Ben to the ambulances."

Introduce? Ben thought that seemed an odd way of putting it.

There was only one ambulance left on standby, all the others already out on missions, but Denis muttered to himself that this was probably going to be all right, and possibly the right ambulance for his new recruit anyway. But best, perhaps, not to mention her little quirks.

The ambulance was smart, sleek, pearly-white and looked brand new. Ben ran a hand over the bonnet. A giggle escaped into the air.

"What was that?" Ben asked.

"Clarissa's ticklish."

Ben looked at Tom as if he were mad. "How can an ambulance be ticklish?"

"You'll find out."

And eventually Ben did, but first he had to admire how up-to-date in every detail this ambulance was – better than anything he had ever seen before. For one thing there was a state-of-the-art communications system on board. Tom flicked a switch and a pleasant female voice announced that she could always be relied on to arrive at exactly the right location and at exactly the right time.

"That's Clarissa."

"Oh!"

"Here's how it works," Tom continued, and began to explain why it was necessary to use a vehicle such as Clarissa to transport patients to the Summerland – a vehicle that looked at any moment in time exactly as they would expect. "Clarissa can shapeshift herself to look like any model or make of ambulance, current or otherwise. Helps the patient to feel comfortable and reassured – some aren't ready to cope with anything else at that point. The presence of an ambulance and ambulance men takes away their need to think through the next step. Death takes people in different ways, or rather people take death in different ways! But it's a recognised fact that not everybody has the same feelings about it. Some will tell you outright that they are still alive and perfectly well and that you can 'shove off' and 'get lost'. Well, we learn how to get around things like that; takes a bit of patience, and some counselling skills. You'll get the hang of it, I'm sure."

"You keep saying that – or rather Denis did." Ben felt at a loss again. Everyone had such high expectations of his capabilities, when he didn't have any at all.

Tom was still trying to inspire him. "A sudden or traumatic death can be very difficult – not everyone knows what to expect - so when you talk to your patients, be casual without losing the efficient touch. A calm, friendly approach is encouraged. Well, you know that already from your Earthly experience. And where appropriate, remember: counsel!"

Ben realised that although he had many years experience under his belt, this new job of his could present some surprises. He hadn't had to deal with departed souls before for one thing. How did you comfort someone who had just lost their grip on an Earthly life, most probably leaving loved ones behind? How did you explain what had happened? *Counsel*, Tom had said. That meant being discreet, gentle, reassuring, but at the same time conveying to the patient that their existence was now headed in a different direction from before and there was no going back. He suddenly didn't feel confident at all.

Tom opened the door to the cabin. "Try it," he said encouragingly.

Ben's well-padded frame sank gratefully into the most comfortable seat he'd ever known. The cabin seemed roomier, too, though from the outside the ambulance looked the same standard shape and size of any vehicle he'd ever used. He looked around for the gear stick and then looked down at the floor, noticing there were no pedals.

"Clarissa does the driving," Tom said. "You just steer. If necessary, that is. The vehicle has all the usual gears, etcetera, but you don't have to worry yourself about when to declutch, brake or anything like that. She does it all automatically. Believe me, when you're out on a run you'll be grateful that you don't have to think about it."

Tom also explained there was a big difference between driving in a reality where gravity kept all four wheels on the ground and driving in one where vehicles had a tendency to hover a few metres off the ground.

"You'll get used to interdimensional travel," he said. "You might feel a little giddy to start with, but that will disappear."

Ben swallowed hard, feeling this was the moment to find out what this vehicle was capable of. "How about a trial run?" he asked.

"Could be arranged," Tom said thoughtfully, stroking his chin in the manner of someone who thinks he has the measure of his new recruit and wants to find out if he is right. "Better still, though, why not start handling rescues straight away?"

"Blimey, don't hang about do you?"

"Just need to do your paperwork, then you can get started. Pop into the office and see Denis, there's a good lad."

Ben filled in the required forms. Denis was a stickler for protocol.

"There's a situation happening right at this moment," the station superintendent said when Ben had finished signing the last official document. "Do you feel up to it? You'll have an experienced partner going along with you, so no need to feel nervous."

Ben did feel nervous. It was almost as bad as his first day out working for the ambulance service on Earth: the adrenalin pumping his heart into top gear, the sweat pouring down his back, fervent prayers that his driving skills would get him through that traffic jam up ahead and enable him to miraculously miss the bollard on the island in the middle of the road. The men he used to work with knew all about ambulances becoming flexible on an emergency - passing through impossible gaps unscathed, leaving the traffic behind them unscathed as well.

He went to climb into the driver's seat. "No need," said his partner in a kind voice. "I'll drive this time."

He was relieved, realising it would give him a chance to acclimatise himself to his new line of work. Maybe it would be a bit like riding a bike, and he'd just click into gear and go on automatic again.

A light on the dashboard was blinking: red for emergency, flashing to green for take-off.

NOW!

The movement was barely perceptible, just a gentle swaying now and again as they hit etheric air currents. "My name's Brian, by the way," said the driver.

"Hi Brian, I'm Ben."

"Yes, I know, mate. Anyway, welcome aboard."

He looked across at the large, well-built, dark-haired, dark-eyed stranger next to him and considered that back on Earth Brian would have been a force to be reckoned with, even though he now seemed to be as gentle and calm as his voice. The physical appearance and the voice just didn't *quite* go together.

CHAPTER 5

Rescue Missions

They were both in uniform. Gone were Ben's jeans and white shirt, though he couldn't remember when exactly he'd taken them off and put this lot on. Now he was dressed in an all-white suit and it felt odd, not at all like the old Air Force-blue serge version he'd once worn back in the 1960s, with its epaulettes and shiny silver buttons, blue shirt and navy blue tie. He still had epaulettes though, these embroidered with an image of a six-pointed star in silver thread. He tried to remember what his uniform had been after he'd transferred from Emergencies to the Control Centre in London. It all seemed a bit vague somehow, no longer important. The move to Control had been his choice. He'd seen enough of accidents and trauma. He realised then how only small pockets of memory were coming back into his mind, though they were all happy memories.

Ben felt good about the way he looked, as if his new clothing had given him a certainty he'd never had about himself before. He put a hand in one of the pockets, only half-surprised to discover his old lucky charm: a small coin, an old silver sixpence. It was of no monetary value, but he had always felt it brought him good luck - irrational really.

A quiet thought to himself. *They think of everything here, don't they!*

"Just come over?" asked Brian.

"Yes, I think so. Can't say I've any idea of time over here, but this is my first outing since leaving the hospital."

"Got you into the swing of things pretty quickly then?"

"Well I used to be an ambulance man so I guess it seemed the obvious choice for me. Sorry, perhaps I should say paramedic, although I never was one of those. That label came after my time."

"Don't worry about labels. We're all from different decades here, so you'd be surprised at some of the differences in job description we get. We all know what you mean."

"I didn't always do the hands-on stuff though – worked at the Control Centre for a few years before retiring. There was a wholesale reshuffle of the service and I opted for a desk job."

"And now you're wondering if what was once second nature to you will have become a little rusty?"

Ben glanced across at Brian. "Too right!"

"It will all come back to you. Everything clicks into place here a lot quicker than anywhere else."

"How long has it been for you?"

"I remember ambulances when they were still horse-drawn!"

Suddenly, and without warning, the ambulance dipped and dropped like a lead weight out of the sky, with Ben hanging onto the dashboard to save himself from hitting his head as he fell forward.

"That's why we wear seatbelts," Brian commented wryly. "Clarissa loves a bit of drama."

With a shriek of brakes and the smell of burning tyres (a bit weird, as they were hovering about five metres above the ground), the ambulance came to a full stop. Ben wound down his side window. Below was absolute chaos. A lorry had jackknifed and hit an oncoming car. Cars behind on both sides had concertinaed into a fine old mess. A police car was already at the scene, the scream of an ambulance not far away. In the distance, the sound of a fire engine in a great hurry.

"Here we go," said Brian, as Clarissa gently lowered herself down onto the road.

For Ben it was just as he'd hoped. All his training came back to him in an instant, though he was totally unprepared for the resistance he was about to encounter.

"That one's yours," said Brian, pointing to the car, and pulling out the stretchers from the back of the ambulance. "I'll get the lorry driver."

The man in the car was definitely a departed person, and his physical body was pinned under an awful lot of crumpled metal; but it soon became apparent that his soul was determined to stay absolutely where it was, stuck to his body with all the stubbornness of a piece of chewing gum on the sole of a shoe. The man was well-dressed. Well, you would be if you were driving a gorgeous, sleek car, slung so low the chassis almost touched the ground.

He looked to be in his early forties. His blond hair was streaked with blood, as was his face. A faded flower hung limply in his buttonhole; the black jacket and pinstripe trousers suggested a wedding. A glance at the passenger seat confirmed Ben's fears - the remains of a grey top hat. Ben guessed the man had been running late. A chance too many, he reflected, having seen many on highways such as this who had chanced their luck. Only for some it never paid off. A sad day, too, for those awaiting the man's arrival.

Ben shook himself free of his emotions. He was an ambulance man and such luxuries were for the moment to be denied, at least until the patient was taken care of.

"Hello, sir," Ben said cheerily, wondering too late if a cheery greeting was really the best approach. The man was already scowling as if the accident was all Ben's fault.

"Don't touch me," he said severely.

"Why?"

"I'm safe where I am. Anyway the fire crew hasn't arrived yet, and we have to wait for them to cut me free."

"Yes, that's true, we could do that. Are you quite comfortable? Any pain?"

"No."

"None at all?"

"No, thank God. Do you want me to have pain?" The man was getting annoyed, interpreting Ben's calmness as somehow not appreciating enough the awfulness of his predicament.

"Well, I'm sorry, but we can't hang around. We have to get the lorry driver to hospital as soon as possible. So are you happy to wait for the next ambulance? I can't guarantee when that will be."

33

Ben couldn't believe what he was saying to the man. Was this being sensitive – helpful even? He couldn't help it though; the words had just come out unbidden. His first day, and his first blunder.

The man looked at Ben, at the ambulance, and at the lorry driver who was even now being carried into the back of the vehicle.

"So you can lift me out of this mess? You don't have to wait for the firemen?"

"No, we don't have to wait. I can have you out in a jiffy."

"Well, that does seem to make more sense than just sitting here, feeling like…"

"Feeling like what?"

"I can't breathe properly… my lungs… I can't breathe!"

"It's ok. You're all right."

Ben kept his voice calm as he reached through what should have been the solid physical mass of a car door, but which was now no hindrance at all to somebody of a different dimension. Taking him gently by his right arm, and supporting his head, Ben lifted the man clear of the wreckage.

"Come on, sir. That's it."

The man glanced briefly at Ben, a flicker of a smile to say 'thank you'. Ben smiled back reassuringly. Brian had the stretcher ready and soon both patients were comfortably ensconced in the back of the ambulance, with Clarissa taking off and away before the fire engine had got to within a quarter of a mile of the scene. With headlights blazing and klaxon blaring (a habit of Clarissa's), unseen and unheard by those on the ground, they travelled across timeless dimensions and landed safely outside the hospital.

"Another two cases for you, Sister," said Brian as they wheeled the trolleys into one of the wards.

"Thank you, Brian," came a voice with a soft Scottish accent. Sister Agnes was a no-nonsense, petite blonde, and a very feminine package of high output energy. She had nerves of steel, which was just as well, seeing the state of some of the cases she had to deal with. The senior nursing Sister smiled at Ben and nodded to him in greeting.

"Nice to meet your partner, Brian. No doubt we'll being seeing a lot more of you in future, young man."

Ben grinned at her, surprised and delighted at her comment, as he'd been a good bit older than a young man when he'd died.

"Thanks, Sister. Glad to be of service."

Brian clapped Ben on the back as they left. "A good day's work, chum. Well done."

And Ben realised it hadn't been that difficult after all.

Ben was glad to get his first mission under his belt. It made a difference to his confidence to know his Earthly expertise had remained intact, though he had to admit helping people across to the Other Side was a very different scenario from being the ambulance man who did everything possible to help them stay in the physical body.

"You managed, then?"

Ben turned to see Horace walking out of the ether, a mist surrounding him that quickly disappeared as his body became more... what could you say? Physical? Solid?

"What... where...? How did you do that?"

"Trade secrets, Ben. I just thought I would drop by to see how you were faring in your new job. You seem to be picking up the threads pretty well."

"Surprised myself, if truth be told, and I am enjoying it so much. Though perhaps I shouldn't say *enjoying* - it's more a sense of fulfilment."

"Ah yes, fulfilment. What a splendid word. And did you used to say that much when you lived on Earth?"

"No, hardly at all, in fact not at all. Never felt fulfilled, well, at least not in the same way that I do now."

"So we can take it that you're perfectly happy to carry on with what you're doing?"

"Oh, yes. Thanks. Couldn't be better!"

"That's all I needed to know. Keep up the good work." And with that Horace disappeared as if he'd never been there. There wasn't even a puff of mist or smoke, or anything. Not a trace.

Ben didn't have much time to reflect on Horace's brief visit, for in the next instant he found he had suddenly relocated to Station One

Two Zero, almost bumping into the station superintendent as he was coming out of his office. Denis was in a hurry.

"Rush job," he said in passing.

"Hang on," said Ben, "anything for me?"

"Nope, and I'm late for a meeting. Can't stop. Quiet day today. Why not take Clarissa out for a trial run? I'm sure she won't mind, and you could do with getting to know her better."

"Why do I need to get to know an ambulance better? Isn't one ambulance the same as another?"

"Not Claris," said Denis. "Anyway she's revved up and ready to go. Don't delay. Never know when you'll be needed back here. Things change all the time."

Ben had nothing else to do, nowhere else calling him urgently, so he automatically picked up a log book and noted his time of departure.

"Ok, Clarissa, let's go driving."

The ambulance gently let go her brakes and glided off into the wide blue yonder. Ben remembered to buckle up. Her take-offs were smooth, but braking... well, that was another matter.

There was no sense of time in this other world, but Ben knew it was a Thursday down on the streets of London below because the radio told him so. He'd been fiddling with the tuning for the last five minutes. Local news headlines were being run through in the same monotone that they always were. Ben could see the traffic building up to a typical rush hour.

He was on his own. There were no emergencies pending; he was just getting in some practice and getting to know his ambulance better. He was about to discover that she had a mind of her own.

"Where would you like to go now, Ben?" said a sweet, ingenuous voice coming out of the dashboard.

"Don't know. What about circling round the M25? Might be something going on there we could help with."

"I don't do traffic jams," Clarissa said with just a hint of sulkiness. Traffic jams were beneath her contempt.

"I know you don't, and I wasn't suggesting you should. Just thought we might send down a little light relief to ease any lurking tensions. You know you're really good at it."

"Ok." The voice was bright and cheerful again.

"Clarissa, how about we get the radio stations to broadcast the right sort of music? You know, the sort that will have people tapping their fingers on the steering wheel instead of punching the horn."

"And how are you going to do that, Ben?" replied Clarissa, with a hint of conspiratorial huskiness.

"Well, let's see. I'm going to need your help of course. But supposing I press one of the buttons on your radio (another old-fashioned favourite of hers) and search around for something suitable. Can you tune in the frequency?"

Ben could see a few drivers already responding, index fingers working in harmony with the strains of *Here Comes Sunshine* by Katie and The Waves.

"That's the ticket," said Ben drumming his own fingers on the steering wheel and whistling softly as he steered Clarissa away from the M25 and towards the M4.

There was, however, just one small problem. Cruising slowly over Heathrow Airport they appeared to be crossing the flight paths of several 'planes taking off or landing. Ben pressed a button on his dashboard and adjusted the tuning until, loud and clear, he heard the voice of the pilot of the intercontinental to New York.

"Did you feel that, Harry? A cold shiver went right up my spine, just as the cabin started to judder. Check with Control that we're still all in one piece."

The co-pilot checked. "Everything's all right. We've still got two wings and the requisite number of engines. Funny that. I felt it too. You ok?"

The captain looked across at his co-pilot as if to say, *I wouldn't be just sitting here if I wasn't!*

"You shouldn't do that you know," Clarissa said in a voice that brooked no argument. "Listening in isn't really allowed. And allowing our dimension to overlap into theirs doesn't help either. No wonder the pilot felt uneasy."

"Sorry, but I couldn't resist it."

"And you could turn off the headlights, too. Draining the battery."

Ben smiled to himself. Was there a battery? Clarissa seemed above such nonsense. An aristocrat of an ambulance, she was very clear about how she wanted the drivers to treat her. Ben couldn't help but ask, "What were you in a former life, Clarissa? A Rolls Royce?"

"None of your business."

They sailed around Middlesex for a minute or two and then a call began to come through from base.

"Emergency on the M4."

On screen the exact location was appearing.

"Three occupants in one car, two in another, one in a third, plus two in a van, and a lorry driver and his passenger. Also a child in the coach, plus the coach driver. All needing assistance. No other ambulances available just yet, though we'll get assistance to you as soon as possible. Can you handle it for now?"

"Yes, we're onto it." But Ben had a sinking feeling this wasn't going to be pretty. And he was on his own.

The ambulance dipped lower and lower, scanning the motorway. Clarissa slowed for a millisecond and then stopped abruptly with a screech of her brakes.

Ben shook his head at her waywardness, glad he'd remembered to buckle his seatbelt. "More like you were a racing car," he muttered to himself.

"Will this do?" asked Clarissa. "I can get closer if you want me to."

Ben quickly assessed the situation down on the ground. There was all the usual chaos of a major accident: a number of ambulances, as well as fire crews, and traffic was backing up along the motorway. Ben knew it must have been hard going for the emergency vehicles to get through. It was raining hard and the surface of the road was slick as grease in a hot frying pan. It took skill and guts to drive in such conditions, especially when people's lives depended on your speed of delivery to the nearest hospital.

He cast his mind back to his own experiences of such moments and remembered what a calm place the cabin of an ambulance could become. A sense of peacefulness, rather than anxiety; something greater than himself taking over the situation, getting him through any sort of difficulties, whether it be traffic jams, failed traffic lights, or low bridges, or even – as once happened – facing a dirty great dustcart that was heading towards him down a country lane with room for only one vehicle. He'd had a seriously injured patient on board, his siren wailing unceasingly, the attendant in the back doing everything he could to keep the person alive, but still the dustcart had kept coming and there was nowhere for either vehicle to go. He could never give anyone a clear answer as to how they'd avoided a collision. Had something shapeshifted the ambulance into another dimension and then back into the material world a minute later? All he could be certain of was that the temperature in the cabin had dropped to several degrees below zero, and that when he checked his rear-view mirror it was to see the dustcart disappearing down the lane behind them, the vehicle brushing the hedges either side...

His mind back on the job, it wasn't long before Ben located those needing to be taken on board. They stood out like a sore thumb, wandering around, forlorn and lost, trying to get the ambulance crew or the fire crew to listen to their pleas for help. Wanting explanations... anything...

"Get as close as you can to that group over there," he said to Clarissa.

While she slipstreamed gently down to a space on the hard shoulder, Ben quickly scanned the group, assessing any injuries that might require the need for a stretcher. He had learned that it all depended on the amount of shock to the spirit as to whether stretchers were needed or not. Physical injuries could pass through to the astral body as a lingering afterthought and that sometimes occasioned the need for a patient to be treated as non-ambulatory, especially if they lost consciousness - their spirit preferring to remain unaware of the existing trauma. Fortunately for him this group were all fully conscious and able to stand on their own two feet. He gathered them together like lost children. They were all still in deep shock.

They were a mixed bunch, all adults except the one little girl. Some of them were dressed as if they had just left work, wearing smart but now crumpled suits. Two of the men wore overalls: a large man and his friend, who had both been in the lorry that had ended up in the middle of the pile of vehicles. They seemed nonplussed to be with this group of complete strangers. The coach driver, normally well-dressed in white shirt, dark trousers and with a smart logo on his epaulettes, was more upset at the present state of his general appearance than anything else that might have happened to him.

"My wife'll kill me," he kept muttering to himself.

Of the women, most were young. Ben hoped none of them had been on their way to pick up children from school, though he couldn't help noticing one of the women kept looking anxiously at her watch. Loved ones always felt the loss of someone dear to them and children were no exception. Ben felt a twist in his heart for the mortal souls who would grieve.

An older woman in the group was looking around her as if searching for someone in particular. Her friend was still back at the scene of the accident, trapped in their car and very much alive. And then there were the two men and one woman standing slightly apart, as if association with the rest of the group might confirm their worst fears. One of the men impulsively took the hand of the young woman. Nothing was said, but it was apparent the human touch was comforting. Ben knew they'd be all right in the end, though he felt some concern for the little girl, still looking forlorn and lost. Her parents were at that moment heading for a London hospital. And there was that pang in his heart again.

He swallowed hard and in a clear voice that meant things were about to be sorted, he said, "Now then you lot, let's see what's what."

A chorus of voices burst forth, wanting to know where they were being taken and what was going to happen to them. Someone pointed to Ben's uniform. "Not local, are you?"

Ben held up his hands as a signal that he needed their patience. "First things first: I'll answer all your questions in good time, but before I do..."

He caught the eye of the older woman in the group and pointed her in the direction of the little girl.

"Take care of her for a mo will you, please? Hold her hand. Yes, that's right. She'll feel better for the contact."

The older woman responded, grateful to be able to do something to help. She smiled reassuringly down at the girl, who smiled shyly back.

"Now, your attention for a moment and I'll explain exactly what has happened and what is about to happen."

His voice was gentle, but commanding, and they all turned to listen, eyes wide with expectation. He cleared his throat, hoping the right words would come.

"You know by now that you have left loved ones behind. For some of you that may include those you were travelling with. They aren't with you because they have survived the accident, whereas you have not."

Most nodded their heads. They weren't stupid. The realisation for some had come more quickly than for others. But they knew.

"Well, I think you won't be disappointed with where you're going, but because of the circumstances of your passing you will all be taken to the Lodge of Rest and Recuperation to start with - our equivalent of a hospital, if you like - and there you will be attended to." A few hands immediately went up as if to question what Ben had just said. "Yes, we have hospitals there, too, only it won't seem the same as any you've experienced before. And you will be cared for until you have regained full health. Some of your recovery will be up to you, for there will have been a certain amount of shock to your soul. It's an emotional thing, that's understood. There will be willing people to help you. Some of you will make the transition to full health quickly, but others may take longer. There's no need to feel a timetable or schedule is attached to your recovery. Everything will happen according to your own needs and in your own good time. Are there any questions?"

"Yes," called a voice from behind Ben. "How do we know this isn't just a dream?"

"You'll come to appreciate that where you're going is so much better than anything you could possibly imagine in a dream."

The whole group looked at him in silence. This was for real, then.

"Now, let's get you sorted and into the ambulance. There's not much space, but perhaps some of you won't mind sitting on the floor, or on each other's laps." There were a few grins from the men.

Clarissa had shapeshifted her rear cabin in an effort to accommodate everyone. It was a tight squeeze, but before she or Ben had time to organise or worry about the seating arrangements, another celestial ambulance was already gliding in beside them.

"Hi, Ben," came the friendly voice. "Jim and I heard you needed some assistance."

"Glad to see you, Brian. As you can see, we're needing a bit of extra space, so any you can take on board would be helpful."

They took half the group each. Most had been strangers to each other, as they had been to Ben, but they were losing their shyness remarkably quickly and seemed at last to trust that, whatever was happening, they were safe with these three men.

Once he'd made sure they were all sitting comfortably, Ben climbed into his driving seat and tapped the dashboard. "Ok, Clarissa, let's go."

The engine roared and up they climbed into the sky until the scene on the ground was out of sight. Clarissa loved this part, when the mission was accomplished and people were safely on board. "Well done, Ben," she thought to herself.

Once they were on course for home, Ben climbed through a hatchway into the back of the ambulance. Time to get to know his passengers better.

CHAPTER 6

Healing

Ben was congratulated on his return to base and he made sure he didn't forget to thank Clarissa, though when he asked her how she'd managed to shapeshift her body when she thought she'd have to accommodate twelve people instead of two, she suddenly lost her voice and became uncommunicative.

"Not giving away trade secrets, eh?"

Clarissa relaxed her brake pads in answer.

Ben kept in touch with some of the people he'd rescued, especially the little girl. She seemed to settle down to her new life with consummate ease compared to the others, who were much older than her and had to make different emotional adjustments. She happened to mention to Ben that she thought she would find it very hard to be apart from her parents, but that had all changed when she realised they could come and visit her at night when they were asleep.

"They never remember in the morning though," she said sagely. "Which is a pity, `cause it would help them to know."

"Maybe one day they will realise," Ben said encouragingly.

"My cat knows," she smiled. "And the parrot."

Ben chuckled to himself. *Trust the parrot to be all-knowing!*

One of the other reasons Ben visited his rescued patients was that it also gave him a chance to meet and talk with the nursing staff. They were the glue that held the place together from the point of view of the patients. Always smiling, always kind, and always a little reminder of the life these souls had left behind – a reminder that was reassuring and familiar. Sister Agnes was the most senior of the Sisters. She had worked at the hospital for a long time and couldn't ever recall a moment when she hadn't been there on the wards, tending the needs of her patients as if they were the most important souls in her care. He thought she was the nearest thing to an angel he could ever hope to meet, and her soft Scottish accent embraced anyone who spoke to her.

A strident voice brought Ben out of his comfortable reverie. It was Denis. "There's a call for you."

"Right-ho," said Ben picking up what looked like a normal telephone, finding it strange to have such an instrument in his hand in a world where everyone – or nearly everyone – was telepathic. However, he was the new kid-on-the-block, so perhaps it was just a convenience made for him until he got the hang of things.

"Hello?" he called down the line.

"Hello, Ben. You won't know me, but thought I'd get in touch. The name's Sam. Have a bit of a job for you. Something different, thought you'd be interested. Heard you were settling in really quickly and besides which Horace thought it would be good experience."

"Um, this job," Ben asked diffidently, wondering what he was letting himself in for, "do I get a say-so about whether I do it or not?" He was beginning to feel he was being thrown in the deep end again.

"Well, yes, I suppose. But I'm sure you won't say no. Will you?"

"Is it a rescue? Or something like that?"

"A bit different from a rescue, actually quite a lot different from what you've done so far. You'll be going to an event that hasn't happened yet, but we want you to be on the spot, so to speak. You will find the experience useful." Sam was being very hazy about details.

"I'm not sure I understand," said Ben. "I'm a bit new here. Are you sure you've got the right guy for whatever this job is?"

"Oh, you'll do," was the answer, as if that closed the matter.

"And you *are* going to let me know what this is all about, aren't you?"

"Oh, yes, as soon as I've done the paperwork."

Ben groaned. Not another Denis!

"Now don't groan," was Sam's sharp response. "It's got to be done proper, otherwise I get into trouble. Can't have that. Won't have that. Perhaps we should meet. Are you free now?"

Ben looked across at the notice board to see if there was a need for him to be on call. Denis caught his eye and shook his head.

"Where shall I meet you?" Ben said down the `phone.

"Well, let's say at the Café Concertina, in the Market Place."

And with that the `phone started to buzz in his ear. Sam had rung off.

"Do you know a Café Concertina?" Ben asked Denis.

"It's on the way to the Halls of Learning."

"Not in the Market Place?"

"No. Sam always gets it wrong. That's a different café. If he didn't have a map sewn into his hat he'd never find his way home."

Ben was beginning to have grave doubts about Sam. He was still wondering why Denis needed to have a telephone. And another thought: he hadn't expected there to be cafés. "Is it self-service?" he asked.

Denis smiled his broadest, friendliest smile and slapped Ben on the back. "Oh, there's no problem with ordering. You just have to think what you want and it appears on the table in front of you."

"But why do people still feel the need to have a drink in a café?"

"Why not? It's sociable, isn't it?"

"Well, yes, I suppose so."

It was a pleasant spot. A gently flowing stream ran down by the side of the café, its banks full of wildflowers, some of which Ben was surprised to find he recognised as having grown near where he used to live. *Used to live!* The thought jolted him. Here he was, having the experience of an altogether different life and yet everything in it seemed ordinary to him – or rather, nothing seemed altogether *out* of the ordinary.

Ben had only just sat down to wait for Sam when he felt a gentle bump against his leg and there was Rufus, tongue lolling out of the side of his mouth as usual, and panting as if he had run a marathon to get there. Ben stroked him all the way from the top of his head to his tail. "Hello, Rufus. Come to keep me company while I wait for Sam?"

"Woof!" came the reply, after which Rufus snuggled down by Ben's feet and went to sleep. This seemed to be the signal for an unusual-looking individual to suddenly appear out of the ether.

Dressed in a brown suit with blue stripes, he stood on the other side of the table. His hair was long and brown, with blue highlights to match his suit. The bottom of his trousers sagged a little around the ankles. His feet were bare.

Ben stood up as the stranger leaned across the table to shake his hand. "Hello Ben, I'm Norman. Sam couldn't make it. Something came up at the last minute, but he sends his apologies and says he'll meet you another time."

Oh, so there'll be another time.

"He has something else lined up for you."

"Oh! Well, it's nice to meet you Norman, but I haven't got a clue what Sam wants me for anyway. He sort of omitted that part. Perhaps you can put me in the picture?"

"In a minute," replied Norman, gesturing to Ben to sit down and taking a seat himself. A glass of orange juice began to coalesce into reality in front of him.

"How did you do that?" exclaimed Ben.

"Everything is just a thought away."

Norman nodded at Ben, encouraging him to do the same. "Reach into your mind, imagine the glass of orange juice, and it will come."

Ben did as instructed and sure enough, in the blink of an eye, the drink appeared. This was easy!

He sat back and sipped his drink, enjoying the pleasant, summery day with just a hint of haze in the distance. Closing his eyes, he felt the peace of knowing there was no need to rush off to do anything in particular. This was... well... *bliss.*

Norman's voice suddenly intruded into his mind.

"In answer to your question about why you and I should meet, Sam had this idea you could be useful in our line of work. And, um, we'd like to borrow Clarissa, too."

Ben opened his eyes and sat up straight. He looked across at Norman wondering what this was leading to. "And your line of work is ... ?"

"We try to heal situations."

"Situations? Not people?"

"No, situations," insisted Norman.

"And the situation you want to involve me in is ... ?"

"There's a conference going on down on Earth. Some good people are speaking. The theme is 'World Unity'. There's bound to be hecklers, though, and the problem is that some of them are likely to become a bit militant. We're going down just in case the situation needs diffusing. Sam thought you might like to join us."

"For the ride?"

"Well, we'll need transport you see, and there might be a scuffle or two to deal with, so you'd be useful, seeing as you're ... "

" ... an ambulance man. Yes, I do see. Well, I'll have to clear it with my station super."

"Oh, he said it's ok with him."

Ben's eyes widened. This telepathy thing was better than mobile `phones any day.

Including Ben and Norman, there were nine in the group. Most of them looked too young and boyish to be responsible enough to heal *any* situation. They crammed themselves into the back of Clarissa as if they were about to embark on a great lark, laughing and joking and jostling each other, while Norman calmly sat up front with Ben. Clarissa shapeshifted her body to accommodate everyone, her hydraulics lifting her chassis an extra few centimetres off the floor to allow for the extra weight. Of course, by Earthly standards nobody weighed anything at all, but from Clarissa's point of view they were substantial, real people, and therefore ... well, it all made sense to her anyway.

Norman had brought a ray gun with him. Ben eyed it suspiciously.

"What do you use that for?" he asked. "Don't hold with weapons myself."

"Oh, it's not really a weapon as such," replied Norman. "It's quite harmless. It sends out rays of harmony rather than pellets of destruction."

"Can't wait to see it in action. Does everyone have one of those?"

"No, just me. The others have their own weapons. All different."

Ben groaned. The others in the back of the ambulance were still behaving as if they were on their way to a party, singing at the tops of their voices.

"Does them good," explained Norman. "Don't worry, we're going to try to *heal* a situation, not *create* a situation. A bit of humour and good feeling gets them in the right mood."

Ben fervently hoped he was right. He knew what young men were capable of getting up to.

Clarissa landed safely just outside the conference hall. It was a large building, set in the heart of the city. Some rich benefactor had built it a hundred and fifty years ago, and its classic frontage did justice to his donation. Ben said he would park Clarissa round the back and wait for them there.

"Park her round the back by all means, but you're coming with us."

"Me? Now hang on, I'm just an ambulance man. I wouldn't know what to do about 'healing situations'. Besides which, perhaps there won't *be* a situation. No, I think I'll stay in the ambulance if it's all the same to you."

"Well, that's a pity, because part of this exercise, Sam considered, would be to show you how we work. He also considered – no, expected – that you'd be interested."

"Why?" asked Ben in a way that suggested Sam must have his head screwed on the wrong way round.

"It's all part of your education."

He knew that settled it. He couldn't say no. Where he was now, after all, was all about being educated and doing something useful.

Clarissa left her motor running. She said it was 'just in case'.

They entered the conference hall as the first speaker was about to approach the podium. At the back of the hall Ben noticed a few flag-wavers. They were all dressed the same as if in uniform: black windcheaters, black jogging pants, black trainers. Various slogans were written on the flags, all stressing their individual views on how they would like to sort out the world's social problems.

So far all seemed quiet enough; there was no ruffling of anyone's sensibilities. Norman and a few of the others had stationed themselves around the hall, sliding in between the aisles, the rows and, where necessary, negotiating around people's legs, completely unseen, unfelt and unheard. One of the group, Tom, sat in the space between two people – well, actually there was no physical space, but he managed to shift enough atoms in the ether to make room for himself. In his hand he held a small object. Ben couldn't quite make it out, except that it was crystalline. Colin was sitting in the centre of the middle aisle, a transparent globe about the size of his hand rested neatly in his lap. He stroked it gently and it started to glow. Three of their group stood behind the people with flags. The first person to stand on the podium began his speech.

Ben expected the man would at the least be heckled; there were bound to be some of the audience ready for some fun, especially the group at the back of the hall, but for the moment everyone remained attentive and quiet. The speaker was talking about world peace, about how each person in the audience could be said to represent the many nations of the world, how the largest nations in the world seemed to have all the say, while the smaller ones were never given a chance, just as some of the people in his audience would never have a choice about the sort of world they wanted to live in; ordinary people were tired of the constant media attention on war, especially, he said, because many people realised there was in fact a lot of good happening around the world. But goodness never became headline news, so negative emotion was encouraged, disempowering the people.

So far, so good.

Then the uniformed group at the back of the hall started to fidget. One voice called out, followed by others, and very soon the air became thick with people's personal feelings. Discontent was suddenly rife. Ben saw it as a whirling vortex of grey matter and it was heading straight for the man on the podium.

"Give it to 'em, Trev!" shouted a voice from the back. "You tell 'em!"

And, as if that was the one spark needed to detonate a battery of ammunition, the speaker acknowledged the call, raising his fist in the air and starting to rant and rave in a loud voice that began firmly enough but ended up on the verge of hysteria.

"Fight for peace, not war! Fight for what you believe in! Get off your backsides and do something, all of you!"

"Yeah!" came the response from the back of the hall. "String up the politicians! We can do without the crooks!"

Some in the audience began to murmur amongst themselves, feeling suddenly vulnerable; words of support became mixed with catcalls and dissent and there was some general heckling from a group nearer the podium. Ben had the impression they were just enjoying contributing to the fracas.

Others stood up, shouting back at the speaker or turning around to say their piece to the audience. It was all getting out of hand. Someone called out "Peace!" as if that one word alone could calm the fractious energy that was threatening to take over. At least one person was brave enough to say that militancy – any sort of militancy – was the quickest way to intolerance and mayhem.

After only a few minutes a riot had broken out at the back of the hall between the group dressed in black and the ushers. Then things got worse as the disturbance spilled over into the main body of the hall, where heated words were exchanged, hands clenched into fists. Chaos reared its ugly head and peace was no longer on the agenda.

The conference had ground to a halt; people's emotions were on a short fuse. Ben glanced in the direction of Norman, who already had his ray gun trained on the centre point of the ceiling, a clear, pearly white ray of light issuing from its muzzle, streaming out and reflecting down to the audience. The others in Norman's group were all standing now, very still. Tom's crystal glowed, as did Colin's globe; and light continued to pour from above, splitting into all the colours of the rainbow, as well as other colours that Ben couldn't name but which he somehow knew were powerful healing rays.

The speaker lost his voice above the hubbub and tried to reach for the glass of water on the podium. He was shaking with emotion, unable to control his feelings, when Norman appeared beside him, laying an invisible hand at the man's elbow, leading him towards a chair on the stage. Suddenly, as quickly as it had started, the disorder and confusion came to an end.

Everything fell quiet, a stillness hung suspended in the air like a wisp of smoke on a windless day, and the audience held its breath. People sat back in their seats, or on the floor, wherever they happened to be. They were stunned. Some glanced around as if they couldn't quite believe what they'd seen or been a part of; others were holding heads in hands, unsure what had hit them. A few bore slight injuries, caused by the panic of some members of the audience but nothing serious, their pride hurt more than anything. More alert members of the audience quickly went to the aid of those who needed them. Some had seen all they needed to and were beginning to leave the hall, shaking their heads in disbelief. Others were using their mobile `phones and dialling 999, conscious of the possibility of further disruption.

Afterwards Ben asked Norman what might have happened if the group hadn't intervened.

"Worse," he replied briskly. "There were enough hotheads in the audience to cause serious trouble and damage. Whether they'd been planted by the opposition or not, who can tell? They could just as easily have been peacemakers who had a slightly warped idea on how to achieve world unity and peace."

"By coercion?"

"Yes. Silly really, isn't it?"

"Maybe Gandhi had the right answer after all."

"He was a good man. But some people want goodness so much they are willing to fight for it. That's the irony and the pity of it. We need more peaceful hearts and minds."

"Any reason why you couldn't have gone in sooner and prevented the violence?"

"The opposition are strong, too - they're a force to be reckoned with."

"By opposition you mean...?"

"Powerful energies that feed off disruptive situations like this. We do our best to balance things out, neutralise. Sometimes our timing is a little out, or so we think. I wonder sometimes whether it works better for the people involved to see the outcome of their actions – just a little – before the resolution. Those powers higher than us would know the answer to that. People will do what people do, sometimes regardless of their better instincts."

"So, that's going to take some time?"

"Perhaps," he replied. He was distracted for a moment or two, his thoughts taking wing Ben knew not where, and then his face cleared and he smiled. "Fortunately, Ben, the people of Earth have a wonderful capacity for bringing out the best in themselves when things get tough. They pull together. We're hoping they'll pull together *before* things get too tough."

"Amen to that."

They all climbed into the ambulance with Ben driving, Norman up front, and a more subdued gang of lads in the back. Clarissa had thoughtfully driven around to the front of the building and had the heater going. They were all feeling chilled to the bone.

"Home, Claris," said Ben, patting her dashboard.

"Would you like some soothing music?" she asked.

"What do you suggest?

"Well, I have whale song, dolphin song, ocean waves on a tropical beach, song birds in a forest...."

"You pick, Claris," said Norman. "I don't think we mind what we hear, as long as it's soothing."

"Right!" she replied enthusiastically.

Loud and clear over the airwaves came the soothing sounds, at full volume, of *We Will Rock You* by Queen.

Everyone began to laugh.

Ben had been asked to meet Horace in the gardens. This could be a debrief session after the excursion with Norman and his group, or perhaps just a chat. Ben never knew in advance what his meetings with

Horace might be about, but he always came away knowing more than he had before.

He found Horace sitting quietly on a wooden bench; birds pecked the ground around his feet, some stopping to glance up now and again at the Great Being as if in silent recognition. Ben stopped a little distance away, not wanting to interrupt what he felt was a chosen quiet moment. Horace's gaze was on the far distant horizon, his stillness that of deep, clear waters whose depths were never ruffled no matter what winds might blow on the surface. The stillness wrapped Ben, too.

Suddenly Horace turned, a welcoming smile on his face. "Ben! Come!"

They sat together on the bench. "How did you find the excursion with Norman?"

Ben was thoughtful for a moment. "I felt uncomfortable at first - just watching without being able to help - but reassured that Norman and his group knew what to do."

"Was it a valuable experience for you?"

Ben nodded. "It showed me how many people here care, even though those on Earth don't always realise it."

"But some know very much what is happening."

Ben was thoughtful for a moment. "Horace, will I be doing more things like that, not just ambulance work?"

"We want you to experience more, yes. Rescues are still important and we still need you to do that as well, but there are many other experiences on offer. You are doing well, Ben. For such a short time here, you are finding your feet very quickly."

"With a lot of help, I have to say," Ben answered.

"There is a lot more in store for you, but we won't push you beyond what you are ready for. No complaints so far?"

Ben laughed at that. "No, absolutely no complaints!"

"Then perhaps soon it will be time for the next step."

Ben looked at Horace as if to say, *So what does that mean?* But Horace was giving nothing away.

CHAPTER 7

Whether You Live Or Not

Clarissa's engine was idling in a parking bay at Station One Two Zero, on standby. Ben was checking his day list with the station super. He'd only been on two missions so far, not counting his sortie with Norman and his group, but already he was feeling like a permanent member of staff. He had landed on his feet, doing the sort of job he was not only good at but which he really, really enjoyed. His enthusiasm was based, he thought, on the fact that helping people had always been at the core of his being. He'd always felt the pull towards reaching out to someone in distress, even if he wasn't sure he might make a difference (though that wasn't true - he had always made a difference).

"Got that?" said Denis, making sure Ben understood exactly where his next assignment was.

"Yes. Thanks. Who's this Malcolm, my attendant?"

"He's new to this, his first assignment since finishing training. He's not had the experience you've had – never been an ambulance man before – but he's keen, so look after him. Get my drift?"

"Sure thing."

Ben checked everything: paperwork, medical kit, blankets, water, tea.

"All in order?" asked Denis.

Ben nodded, and turned to leave.

"Hang on a minute." Denis wasn't finished with him. "I'm curious to know about your trip with Norman and his crew. How was it?"

"Revelatory," was all Ben was prepared to say.

"Learned something then?"

"Yeah, lots."

It had been a lot to take in. He was learning the basics about how his world connected with the Earthly one he'd come from and that there was some sort of two-way traffic going on most of the time, but in all his previous life he'd never heard about the work of such people as Norman. It made him wonder what else there was that he didn't know about yet!

He slid into the driver's seat and buckled up, glad to be back in Clarissa for a normal day's work. The practice of healing situations was perhaps not for him, though he remembered Horace's words about the experience being valuable. But it had been difficult. He'd felt powerless, only being able to observe rather than getting involved. Basically, he preferred to be a hands-on man.

Ben had to give credit where it was due. Norman and his group were good, though he realised they had had to carry the burden of responsibility, making sure the outcome was a positive one. There was no rule book, they just had to use their intuition and skills as they saw fit. It had been a sobering experience.

His attendant climbed into the seat beside him and Ben was suddenly and fully back in ambulance mode.

"Hello, Malcolm, I'm Ben. This is your first time, I understand."

"Yeah," replied a slightly nervous voice with a broad Aussie twang.

"Don't worry, the nerves will go once we're airborne. A little hint - fasten your seat belt."

Malcolm looked bemused, but did as he was told. Clarissa allowed herself a small inward smile as she took off, rising in a gentle ascent, levelling out and then dipping gracefully through the misty veil that separated the Earthly world from hers.

"Been over long?" Ben asked, hoping conversation would ease Malcolm's nerves.

"No. And they don't waste much time getting you into the swing of things, do they?"

Ben grinned.

"How long for you?" asked Malcolm.

"Oh, probably a parsec longer than you."

Malcolm smiled. "So that's what, a heap longer than me, or just a thought longer?"

"Somewhere in between, but not long, no. I was lucky, found my feet pretty quickly once I'd come out of the hospital. Doing the work is what helps."

"They said that would happen, you know, that work gets you right into the thick of things. It's just I didn't quite envisage doing this."

"Did you have an easy time of it ... ?"

"What, passing over?"

"Yes."

"It was a bit drawn out, but I don't remember any of the pain now."

"Perhaps you'd rather not talk about it."

"No, don't mind. My guardian says it's good for me to reflect and put everything into perspective, see the reasons for how my life turned out the way it did."

Ben hadn't heard the word *guardian* used until now. Perhaps Horace was his guardian? *Horace!* The name still didn't really fit. He puzzled over it briefly, then dismissed it abruptly – other things to think about right now.

"So your Earthly life was difficult?" he said.

"Not all of it, but I made mistakes," replied Malcolm.

"Oh, join the club. I know all about those. So you've begun your counselling sessions, then?"

"I'm choosing when to have them, now things are getting clearer. How about you?"

"Yep, just one or two so far, but I've found it really does help."

Ben remembered how in one session with Horace his mind had been opened up to the positive things that had come out of his previous life, which he'd been encouraged to consider as well as those occasions when he hadn't been quite so positive or responsible. There was still such a lot to learn about himself.

"Eh-up," said Ben suddenly. "Something's happening. Clarissa?"

"Signal coming in," she said in her crisp, clear tones.

"I'm on to it," replied Ben, patting her dashboard in thanks for her acute observation.

Below them lay a wide expanse of countryside, then a village and a small row of houses, and then one in particular. Clarissa pulled up with her usual suddenness. Malcolm lurched forward and then back. He was a dirty shade of pale, but grateful that he hadn't somersaulted through the windscreen.

"See what you mean, mate," he grunted.

"All right, Claris, That's enough showing off. Right, Malcolm, it looks as though we're just in time. You take over the wheel. I'll see to this."

A man and woman, paramedics, were carrying a stretcher out of the house. Ben picked up his bag and followed the stretcher into the back of the Earthly ambulance. The doors shut behind him and the muffled voices up front told him the crew had already settled into the driver's cabin.

With Malcolm's help, Clarissa positioned herself alongside the other ambulance, with oncoming traffic oblivious to her presence. Well, almost. She could hear passing motorists commenting: "God, it's cold in here! Close the windows!"

"They are closed," several passengers chorused, while their drivers turned up the heating and accelerated as if that was going to help remove them from the freeze zone more quickly. They soon slowed down, however, looking tentatively skywards as they tried to work out whether or not their unease was perhaps due to being the object of a police surveillance helicopter.

"Right," Ben muttered under his breath. "Let's see what we have here."

He pulled back the blanket covering the inert body to reveal the face of a young man, probably no more than twenty years old, fair hair above what might have once been a handsome face. He was glad Malcolm wasn't seeing this. Opening his bag he pulled out what to all intents and purposes looked like an ordinary stethoscope and began examining the young man's chest, stomach and abdomen. "Hmm," he muttered to himself. "Didn't help yourself, did you?"

The young man's eyes fluttered and then were wide open.

"Who're you?" asked a voice with no substance, thin and cracked.

"Who do I look like?" answered Ben, pointing to his uniform which had conveniently changed into something the lad would have found more recognisable than a pure white suit.

"Oh, a paramedic."

"Yes… with a slight difference." This said in a muttered undertone.

The young man had closed his eyes again.

"Come on, mate, wake up. We haven't got all day."

The young man opened his eyes again. "What do you mean, we haven't got all day? You're taking me to hospital."

"Yeah, but not your local one."

"It's serious then."

"Oh, yes! It's deadly serious."

And then a light bulb went on in the young man's head, and he said, "I did it then?"

"You sure did. That's why I'm here."

Suddenly the young man looked alarmed. Although he hadn't worked out how it was possible for a paramedic to exist in the same nebulous realm as himself, there was another more pressing question on his mind. He tried to sit up. "What's going to happen to me now?"

Ben looked at him with great sympathy. Suicide was always a difficult subject to tackle. Every case was different. What could he say? Hopefully, Sister Agnes would have a chance to talk to the young lad. She would be diplomatic, gentle and calm about it all, but also honest about what came next.

Out loud he said, "Don't worry. You'll have a meeting with a lovely lady called Sister Agnes. She'll sort you out."

"Oh, good. I mean that is good, isn't it?" the young man said nervously. Ben nodded. "This all seems very strange, though. And what's that awful smell?"

"You, mate. You'd been in that house for a couple of weeks before anyone found you."

"Oh God, what a mess."

"You could say that."

The young man lay back on the stretcher, tears welling up in his eyes.

"I was desperate, see. I couldn't find another way out. I was no good to anyone. I have no family… Well, that's not exactly true. I do have a family but we've not kept in touch, if you see what I mean."

Ben tucked the blanket more firmly around the young man and sat down beside him.

"Bit of a black sheep were you?" he said kindly.

"Yes. A bit of an OTT black sheep! Oh God, what an awful life."

"It's ok. I do understand what life can be like. It isn't easy, and perhaps for you it was more difficult than for some."

"So what comes next? I mean what will this Sister Agnes say, or do?"

"I can't tell you. It's not my department. I just pick up and deliver."

That wasn't absolutely true. Ben was learning to have exceptional skills above and beyond his calling, as well as being good at picking up and delivering.

"You know what I regret most?" said the young man.

"No."

"I've never been in love."

"That's a pity."

"I would have liked to have known what it was like, see."

"Yes, I do. Love is something not to be missed."

"But I've missed it now haven't I?"

"There's plenty where you're going."

"But it won't be the same as… well you know what I mean. They don't do that sort of stuff where we're going, do they?"

"It's different, you're right," said Ben, not sure if he really knew what he was talking about anyway. "But don't worry, there'll be other opportunities in the future."

"What, another chance?"

"Always another chance. We don't always make the right choices, but there are opportunities to make other choices… whenever."

The young man closed his eyes for a moment, saying softly to himself, "I just want to experience love. Just once."

Ben took the young man's hand and held it firmly. "I'm taking you into another ambulance. Just lie back and relax. You'll feel a slight wobble and we'll be there before you can blink an eye. What's your name by the way?"

"Tony."

"Ok, Tony, here we go."

The image of Ben and the young man began to glisten and vibrate, molecules separating, and then coming together once more. They were on board Clarissa. Ben gave his patient a sleeping draught, making sure he was comfortable. Tony's physical body lay where he had left it, covered in a blanket at the back of the other ambulance.

Ben then joined Malcolm up front. "Where are we, Malcolm?"

"Just crossing the Northumberland coast, mate, heading out to sea."

"Perfect. Hit the accelerator."

Ben caught up with Sister Agnes later and asked after Tony. She said he was doing very well and acclimatising himself to being in a different reality.

"The only thing I haven't told him is about the next step."

"His eventual return to Earth, you mean?"

"Yes."

"But he's having a lot of help, knowing that there's the chance to experience something better, a new and more positive life."

"He said he just wanted the chance to experience love, the Earthly kind that is."

"Poor wee soul," she sighed. "Life on Earth doesn't get any better. For all its new-fangled technology and so-called easier way of life, it isn't any easier. But this future life of his will perhaps be the opportunity to find the love he seeks."

Ben nodded. The life he'd once known was hard, but he had found love and that had made all the difference. Life had also been full of the unexpected and that was happening here, too, though there weren't any hard bits as far as he could see. Not knowing why he hadn't met his parents yet was still a bit confusing.

"Don't worry, you'll see them in due course," the Sister assured him. "There's a reason, but not one you need to worry about."

Ben smiled lopsidedly at her, a smile that didn't quite reach into all the corners of his heart. But he did feel reassured.

And then she disappeared, and he found himself back at Station One Two Zero.

Nothing about the Summerland was ordinary.

★

CHAPTER 8

The More There Is To Know

Horace was in Denis's office. They were chatting about the benefits of Cloud Nine over Cloud Seven. Ben thought they must be joking. "There is no Cloud Nine or Seven," he said.

"Ah, but there you're wrong," said Horace. "The view from Cloud Nine is vastly superior to that from Cloud Seven."

Denis burst out laughing, leaving Ben to wonder if they were both crazy.

Horace harrumphed to clear his throat. "Ben, we must talk."

Denis gave a nod that said Ben was free and not to worry about any incoming missions. "Education is just as important as rescue missions, lad," he added.

Oh no, not that again!

Horace put his arm around Ben's shoulders and steered him in the direction of the Gardens of Remembrance, choosing a sheltered spot under an almond tree, where the vista spread itself out before them in varying shades of amber and gold, mixed in with some subtle hints of apple green.

"Ben, you've been here a little while now..."

"It doesn't seem very long," answered Ben, thinking that Horace's words seemed to be leading to an announcement of future responsibilities that he really wasn't ready for. He needed more time.

"But it is long enough for us to have a chat about important things, for you to understand more about this new world you live in."

"I haven't heard it called that before. A world? To me the Summerland is just a place."

"Ah, a place, yes. But a place like no other. And there are several of them."

"Several of what?"

"Places. Dimensions. You see, you are existing in only one of these dimensions. This is not all there is. Dimensions lie above and below this very place, this reality. And they are all very real to those who live in them."

"You said above and below...?"

"*As above, so below* is a well known saying, I believe; and it is true, but the *above* is not an exact reflection of what is *below*. However, you would be able to understand, I think, that *above* suggests a higher form of existence, whereas..."

"*Below* is a lower one?"

"Yes. However, for today we will not be talking about specific dimensions. I just want you to understand that where we are now is not the only dimension in this reality. You have realised Earth is third-dimensional, whereas we are not. We are the next level up."

Ben nodded. That much he *could* understand.

"As dimensions move upwards they become more and more refined, refined to the point of a greater and greater lightness of being."

Ben listened intently to what Horace was saying. He had never considered whether there would be other dimensions. He had just always thought of there being just one big dimension, but it seemed there were portals, doorways, veils, that separated one dimension from another.

Horace went on to explain that if, for example, someone from a higher dimension wished to communicate with someone from a lower one, they would have to reconfigure their dimensional reality.

"How do they do that?" Ben asked.

"You have experienced yourself recently an occasion where a patient of yours had to be transported from one place to another, as well as you."

"Oh, you mean Tony?"

"Yes. Were you not aware of how your vibration changed as you transferred from the physical reality of an Earthly ambulance to that of Clarissa?"

"Well, it all happened so quickly. We just transferred. I didn't think about it at the time, but there was a sort of tingling, an effervescence. That's the only way I can describe it."

"It is not quite the same when someone transfers from a higher dimension to a lower one, but it will give you some idea of how, when the occasion demands it, our vibrational body can transform from one situation to another. Higher Beings must cloak themselves in denser matter in order to relocate to a lower dimension. Depending on how high the dimension is they are coming from, will determine how many times they must go through another veil to harmonise with the next dimension."

"What about the other way round?"

"No-one can transfer from a lower dimension to a higher one until they are ready, until their spiritual body can accommodate a finer vehicle. It is a process that must be earned."

Ben looked thoughtful for a moment. "So it is possible to transfer from one dimension to another. Does this happen for any particular reason?"

"Transference happens when there is a need. Sometimes there is a great need for a Higher Being to work at a lower dimension. It all depends on requirement."

Ben was thoughtful for a moment, trying to absorb the fact that Higher Beings chose to come down to a lower dimension in order to help those in need. "They heal situations, too, don't they?"

"Yes, they can help in any situation. And it is a great sacrifice, for it is not a simple matter to leave their level of vibrational reality to enter a reality that is several levels lower. It takes a Master to be able to descend to a much lower dimension. It is a question of holding the vibrational energy in perfect harmony."

"I can imagine how difficult that must be."

"But it is what they choose to do. Later, Ben, you will learn more about this, but for the moment what I have said is enough for you to think over."

"Thank you. It is certainly making me realise how little I know, and how much more I *want* to know."

"Come, I wish you to see something."

Ben followed Horace along one of the many paths that led in and out of the Gardens of Remembrance. It seemed that in only the twinkling of an eye they were both standing in a part of the garden that was new to him. A fountain played a fine spray over a large water lily pond. The water touched Ben's cheek, and when he put his hand to his face he realised his skin was still dry. "I'll never get used to this," he murmured.

"It is all to do with vibrational energy. Here in this dimension you fit perfectly with all that is around you. Therefore, even the water in the fountain's spray is the same frequency as yourself. That's why it doesn't make your skin the slightest bit damp."

"And I suppose that's why at some point..."

"When you are ready..."

"...I won't need to go to the Café Concertina to have a drink, because my body will be in perfect sync with everything around me and Earthly habits will have melted away."

"But it would be a pity not to go there just to socialise."

"Yes," Ben grinned. "It's a great place for that."

"Now, Ben, you have learned a little more than you once knew."

"Well, if this is the education you've spoken of then I'll enjoy every moment of it."

"There will be much more and it will be varied but, yes, it will all be enjoyable."

Horace laid a hand on Ben's shoulder, with a look in his eyes that said he had to be somewhere else, but that Ben would never be far from his thoughts. "We will meet again soon. Little and often I think would be good."

And with that he disappeared, leaving Ben to mull over what he had just learned.

Back at the ambulance station, Ben's mind was still full of different dimensions and vibrational synchronicity. With still so much to learn and understand, his mind felt it would be handy sometimes to have a crochet hook of sorts to unpick the tangles in his brain. He had to admit, though, that where he was now had become much more real to him than his former life had ever been. Here there were no hidden scenarios or dilemmas; here he felt alive.

In his old life, his ageing body had quibbled non-stop at doing shift work; there were always problems with lack of sleep, his body never happy to submit to odd working hours. Now he was always full of energy and yet happy to have quiet moments of doing nothing in particular - though being an ambulance man meant he had to be available at a moment's notice if there was a job to be done. But that never bothered him in the slightest, not now.

There were no drawbacks in his job, even if it included dealing with an independently-minded ambulance called Clarissa. Ben loved her for all her little idiosyncrasies, and she loved him for all of his too. With him she was always all sweetness and light, even though sometimes her idea of sweetness and light was somewhat different from his! The other ambulance men thought Ben and Clarissa must have a special bond, as she never gave them the same respect.

He cast his eyes up at the noticeboard to check whether any missions needed a crew. It was a busy time. His name was there as the next on the list, curiously with no other name next to it. A light flickered, heralding new information coming through. His mission, it seemed, needed only half a crew. Time to get moving.

Clarissa was on standby and had already begun warming up her engine. "Good girl," said Ben. "You knew I was coming."

They took off smoothly in a graceful arc that lifted them clear of the ether, sliding down gradually through a cloud-darkened sky. Around them thunder and lightning were wreaking havoc in a land criss-crossed by small country lanes; here and there fallen trees blocked pathways and all the while leaves, twirling in a never-ending dance, whipped through the air until they became so rain-soaked they collapsed into waterlogged ditches or collected in drifts along the edges of the lanes.

"Can you see anything through this murk?" called out Ben.

"Not much," Clarissa replied. She banked hard to the left and straightened out, moving lower and lower until she hovered about five metres from the ground.

"Swivel around a bit, Claris. Maybe we'll pick something up despite the rain." At that moment it was teeming so hard Clarissa was convinced it must be putting dents in her bodywork.

"Go back, go back," shouted Ben. "There, cast your beams *there!*"

The ambulance steadied herself in the buffeting wind and shone her headlights into the gloom on high beam. "I see what you mean. Could be somebody. Their shapes look fairly human."

"Then jump to it, Claris."

She allowed herself to drift in the fierce air towards the human-like forms, descending until her wheels were only a whisper away from terra firma. Applying her brakes firmly, she rooted herself to the spot, even if it was an airborne one.

"Good girl. Stay put. I'll manage from here."

"Shall I heat up some water?"

"Mmm, you'd better. They might be feeling a bit chilled."

A small pulsing light appeared on Clarissa's dashboard to indicate the kettle had been switched on.

Ben hauled himself out of the driving seat along with his kitbag of etheric medical supplies. As he took a few more steps, the mist surrounding the shapes began to clear, revealing a man and a young girl, dry as a bone, but shivering - not with cold, but with shock. Two very confused people.

Sitting on the grass verge they looked at Ben with some surprise and not a clue of how they had got there. Both cast an uneasy glance in the direction of their car, which was now firmly wedged into the trunk of a large oak tree. Extraordinary as it seemed, they had managed to jump free of their physical bodies before the crash, with no memory of pain or injury. Their shock was due only to the suddenness of their departure, which had been caused by an oil slick at the exact spot where the car's tyres, wet from hitting a puddle, had planed across the road, the man losing control of the steering.

Ben explained, as best as he could, why he was there and what had happened. The man shook his head in dismay, explaining how he had been driving his daughter Lily to visit one of her friends. She was supposed to be going to a party. "A party!" he mumbled in despair, as if that was no good reason to be in the situation he was in now.

It was the shock talking and Ben knew a way to make him feel instantly more comfortable. He sat the man at the back of the ambulance and cocooned him with warm blankets; a fresh pot of tea was soon brewing and a steaming cup put into hands that were getting steadier by the minute. It was a beverage guaranteed to work as well in Ben's dimension as it did down on Earth, calming the nerves and giving the hands something to do. The man cupped the warmth and sighed quietly with relief. Lily, meanwhile, overcoming her shock very much more quickly than her father, had sat herself up front in the driver's seat and was currently conversing freely with Clarissa, who clearly enjoyed the young girl's company. She was explaining to Lily how the navigation system worked.

"It's like this, you see, Lily, I just hone in on a certain wavelength, which has a particular colour. Let's say it's orange. That tells my navigational system where to go, it gives me a precise location. I just log on to that beam and go!"

"Wow, that's cool," said Lily. "Do you have other colours, you know, that tell you to go and do different things?"

"Well, there's the purple beam that says there's already an ambulance on its way and not just me. Then I need to communicate with the other ambulance and ask them if they need back up. You know, that sort of thing. And then there's the blue ... "

Lily looked back at her Dad, who was still talking to Ben. "And what does Ben do?"

"Oh, he's just the driver," said Clarissa with an air of finality that said she didn't think this conversation should be about Ben. Luckily Ben hadn't heard her, or else she knew he'd be telling the girl a slightly different story.

As he was talking with Lily's Dad, Ben was thinking how lucky it was that he and his daughter had been able leave their bodies before the accident had reached its final conclusion. Although in shock from the experience, Lily and her father were otherwise quite ok, only very sad that they'd left behind a grieving wife and mother.

Ben tried to reassure the father by saying, "Later, perhaps you could try to communicate with your wife. Let her know you're ok."

"What do you mean?"

"Well, think about it. You're still fond of her, still love her, and she still loves you. Don't you think she'll be able to pick up your presence and recognise it? "

"What, you mean just float down and watch her cooking dinner, doing the dishes, and expect her to know I'm there?"

"Yes, it's worth a try, isn't it?" Ben persevered. "Don't discount her feelings. She may be more in tune with you than you think. Women especially have a knack for these things. And believe me, it *can* help her."

"How?"

"You will find out, when you're ready," was Ben's cryptic comment, although if he was honest with himself he didn't know *how* it would work for this man; he just knew with a certainty that continued to grow and grow that anything was possible. You just had to believe. The trick was whether those down on Earth were open to such help. A loving presence had to be helpful, surely! He hoped it helped his Linda. She was often in his thoughts and whenever he could he would visit her, drifting with ease through the veils that separated his world from hers. If he was honest, it helped him too.

The man looked at Ben. He hadn't the slightest idea about his future now or what was in store for him and his daughter, or even where he was going next. When he'd been *alive* it had been routine, straightforward: get up at 6.30 a.m. and have breakfast, get the train, go to work, train back home, dinner, watch TV after reading his daughter a bedtime story, and then bed. That was it. So what now? Was this Heaven, or somewhere else, somewhere in between? A ghost land perhaps? Here he was sitting in the back of an ambulance talking to someone who'd told him he'd died, while his daughter sat up front chatting with a very talkative ambulance. How weird was that?

Reading his mind, Ben said, "There's nothing to fear. You left fear behind when you came over and now it's time to get you to where you're supposed to be."

Ben took the teacup from the man and encouraged the daughter to sit with her Dad while he drove Clarissa out into the far blue yonder, a beam of light guiding them to their destination.

"An interesting case," remarked Clarissa quietly, once they were airborne.

"Yes," said Ben thoughtfully.

"I really like Lily. Do you think she'll keep in touch?"

It wasn't like Clarissa to make attachments to those she helped rescue. Ben touched her dashboard reassuringly. "Sure to," he said.

As they had sailed through the mists of time, Lily and her father held each other's hands, talking quietly, reassuringly. Ben couldn't quite make out if it was Lily doing the reassuring or her Dad.

Finally, they touched down outside the Lodge of Rest and Recuperation where Sister Agnes was already waiting, her starched white uniform lending an air of comforting reassurance.

"Hello, Ben. Thank you. I'll take it from here," was all she said as she took the daughter's hand and the arm of the father, and led them through to the ward, turning at the last moment to look at Ben with a twinkle in her eye and a reassuring grin. Ben smiled back. She was an efficient lady and the patient always came first.

"Time to head back to base, Claris. And sometime soon I'm going to give you a good clean and polish."

"Promises, promises," she muttered.

Later, Ben related the case to Horace. Horace made no comment, only nodding sagely at the ease of passing for the father and daughter.

"I tried to keep the situation as normal as I could, say things that I thought would help. But it felt odd because I really don't have that much experience of these things."

"You *do* have the experience though," insisted Horace. "Not only from what you have been learning in this dimension, but also through your experiences of your Earthly life. You learned more about people then than you realise. Don't deny what you know, Ben."

"If I'm honest I don't know how this man will adjust to his new life, or whether he'll listen to what I said about tuning into his wife. But anything is possible. I do know that."

Horace looked steadfastly at Ben, a look that was full of meaning.

"You're learning all the time, and sometimes things are not always clear, but your focus is always to help. That is good. It is not necessary always to have the answers to everyone's questions. The man will not immediately understand everything about why what has happened has happened, or even what now lies in store for him and his daughter. His Earthly life was full of routine, straightforward. Now his life is suddenly turned around. How long was it before he realised what had happened?"

"Well, to begin with he wasn't sure if he was a ghost caught somewhere in between worlds. I know how strange this world can feel when you're new to it. I'd only just left the hospital when I found myself talking to an elf!"

Horace chuckled. "You met Hendrish, then."

"You know him?"

"Yes, he has a habit of meeting those who have been newly discharged. Did he try to enlist you?"

Ben nodded. "He offered me a job in a laboratory."

"He means well," said Horace, smiling. "Oh, and just so you don't offend anyone, Hendrish is not an elf, he's a gnome. Elves are much taller."

"The little girl, Lily," Ben mused. "Clarissa seems to have made a friend."

Horace smiled. "Clarissa has a gentle heart."

"Mmm," Ben agreed, realising perhaps for the first time that she did!

CHAPTER 9

Angels Can Be Insistent

Clarissa loved having a good clean and polish.

Her engine purred with delight as she called out, "Ooh, just a little to the left. There, that's it. Ooh, that feels much better."

"You've got a bit of a dent there, Claris. What have you been getting up to on my day off?"

"Oh, it's that Malcolm. Misjudged coming in to land and one of the other ambulances couldn't get out of the way fast enough. Matilda wasn't half cross!"

"I'm sure you tried to smooth things over with her. Didn't you?"

"Well, her bumper was a bit out of whack, but she could see I hadn't got off scot-free either. We blamed it all on Malcolm anyway."

"Poor chap."

"I think he was sorry afterwards. He was in quite a state when he got back from our mission."

"What on Earth were you up to?"

"Well, we were unprepared and it was a difficult rescue. Some people got trapped and they took a bit of convincing about our reason for being there. I helped," she added brightly.

"How did you convince them?"

"I'd just started to talk to them - you know, in a nice friendly way - and that was when they all realised they were either living in a fairy tale where ambulances had voice boxes, or they really had passed over. It was easier after that. But Malcolm found it a challenge. He's still quite new to the job, isn't he? I tried to talk him through it, but he's gone to see Denis. He's in his office right now, getting a debrief."

"I'm sure you did your best Claris. It couldn't have been easy for Malcolm, seeing as he's fairly new to this sort of thing. Who did he have with him?"

"No-one. Just me. That's why it was so hard for him. We were only out for a practice run."

Ben remembered his own solo experience on a practice run.

He met Malcolm just as he was coming out of Denis's office and in less time that it takes to say 'Would you like a drink?' they were at the Café Concertina. "Heard you were caught unawares," said Ben, stirring his coffee.

"I didn't handle it very well."

"You got everyone out, though?"

"Not a problem with that, but… well, I don't know how you managed it when you were on Earth. It must have been a hundred times worse."

"I know it sounds unsympathetic, but you do get used to detaching yourself, eventually. You have to. No time to think about your own feelings. It's the same here I guess, only at least here their sufferings have come to an end. Remember that."

"I think that was the problem. I thought they were still suffering and I knew I couldn't make them better. Felt so helpless."

"Don't beat yourself up about it. Before you came here you'd never done anything like this before. At least I had some experience up my sleeve. Anyway, what made you decide to do ambulance work? Big change from what you were used to?"

"I used to work in an office, but I'd always had a hankering to join the ambulance service. Never had the guts to do the training and face the reality, if you see what I mean."

"So, that's why you've chosen to do it now you're here?"

"Well, I got a bit of advice."

Ben smiled. He could imagine how the advice was given. "They gave you several suggestions, but helped you make up your mind?"

"You could say that. But I was really happy with my decision. Can't fault them for that."

Ben had an idea, well, more of an inspired thought. He just wasn't sure where it had come from. "When you've finished your drink we'll go back to the station and Clarissa and I will take you out for a ride."

"Isn't that asking for trouble?"

"Look, I know Clarissa has a reputation for homing in on trouble spots, but she's really conscientious, that's all. I'll talk to Denis and we'll make sure this is just a pleasure run. No hidden missions."

Malcolm needed some persuading, but eventually he and Ben were buckled up in Clarissa's cabin and heading off into the wide blue yonder in search of a pleasant adventure.

"Ok, Claris, we're open to suggestions."

"Do you think that's wise?" whispered Malcolm.

Clarissa coughed and interrupted. "I know what to do. I've got my orders. No accidents, just a relaxing day out. I thought perhaps a glide over the Alps might be nice. What do you say boys?"

Ben and Malcolm grinned, and agreed – as long as the weather was good. "What time of year is it down there?" asked Ben. "Check on the weather, will you, Claris?"

"Okey-dokey," came the cheerful reply. Clarissa seemed to be enjoying the chance to play.

They sailed above the snow-capped mountains, pink in the early morning light. It was a glorious sight, and Malcolm immediately began to feel better. He opened his side window and took a deep breath. "Fresh air. Lovely."

"Blimey, Malcolm, it's a bit cold."

"Oh, sorry." The window was closed.

This was the life. What could possibly go wrong on a day like this? The three of them were revelling in the absolute bliss of the blue sky, the sunshine and the silent mountainscape they were passing over. Even Clarissa's revs had slowed down to the barest whisper.

But relaxed as she was, Clarissa was always alert to possible changes and Ben noticed a light flickering rapidly on the dashboard.

"What is it Claris? Something amiss?"

She coughed to hide her embarrassment. "We have a passenger on board, in case you haven't noticed."

Just then a voice came from behind, "Bit cramped isn't it?"

They both turned round at the same time to be met with the frank stare of a complete stranger.

"Just down there will do."

"Where?" enquired Ben politely. Well, you would be polite to a figure dressed all in white, surrounded by a halo of golden light.

"Right down there."

Malcolm nodded to Ben that he should just get on with it and do as he was asked and start lowering Clarissa down to the ground. The fact that they were halfway up a very tall mountain was not discussed.

"Thank you. That will do nicely. Now perhaps you will follow me," said the angel. "And please bring your medical kit."

"It's freezing, Ben!" shouted Malcolm, as he stepped out of the ambulance.

"No time to think about that. Anyway you're just imagining it. Think of yourself as wrapped in a bubble of warm sunshine."

"Please hurry," urged the angel. "He hasn't got long and the rescue party is still too far away."

They followed the angel's guiding light as she made her way towards a small dark patch in the snow. A hazy, sprite-like figure hovered close by, a silver cord still connecting him to his physical body.

"Looks a goner to me," muttered Malcolm as he knelt down beside the man.

"Can't be," said Ben, "otherwise Miss Angel here wouldn't be around. And the silver cord's still attached to his body, which means he's not ready to go yet. There's hope. Let's get to work."

In no time at all Malcolm had placed a mask over the dying man's face. Flicking a switch in the medical kit, the etheric equivalent of oxygen began to flow steadily into the man's lungs. At the same time, Ben was injecting something into the man's arm. The angel nodded that she approved.

Both ambulance men worked seamlessly together. Slowly the vital signs of life returned to their patient and the injured man started to moan.

"That's a good sign and no mistake," remarked Malcolm.

"Keep up with the oxygen, Mal. He's still not stable."

Ben reached into the medical kit again and pulled out a small, folded piece of soft fabric. He shook it once, then again, several times. Each time the fabric increased in size until it was big enough to cover the whole of the man's body.

"No good putting him in the ambulance," said Ben, "his particle energy wouldn't match Clarissa's, but this will keep him warm. Special quality this, completely invisible to any but us. He'll feel a lot more comfortable now."

"I guess the rescuers wouldn't be expecting to see an ambulance up here anyway," grinned Malcolm.

"Get a bit of a shock," Ben agreed.

By this time colour was returning to the man's face and warmth to his body. His eyes flickered, but only for a moment. The guardian angel placed a hand on his forehead and he promptly lost consciousness again.

"Better that way," she said. "His body will feel pain soon enough when he comes to."

Close by they could hear voices. The rescue team had arrived. Ben, Malcolm and the angel drew back and watched as the rescuers, hardly believing their luck that the man was still alive, carefully eased him onto a sledge-stretcher.

The angel turned to the ambulance men and gave her thanks. "It was not time for him to depart," she said. "He still has work to do, dreams to fulfil. Thank you for being here when I needed you." And with that she was gone.

As the rescuers began their descent, their patient firmly strapped to his stretcher, a halo of light hovered over them.

"Not letting him out of her sight then?" said Malcolm.

"Never will, I guess. I've seen a light like that before you know, only never realised what it was, always thought it was my imagination. But when they've just been talking to you, well…"

Malcolm laughed. "Yes, it's hard to ignore them then."

Ben laughed too and clapped his partner on the shoulder. "That was a good day's work, but I'm parched. Let's go celebrate with a cup of tea."

Clarissa had the automatic tea-maker switched on and the water had almost boiled when they got back to the ambulance. Over their steaming mugs they watched as the sun began to dip below the mountaintops, its rays turning the snow to pink and gold.

"Thanks, Ben," murmured Malcolm. "I feel a lot better now."

Clarissa's front bumper curled into a broad smile. She couldn't wait to tell Denis all about it.

Ben was in Denis's office. Papers lay strewn all over the desk and he wondered briefly if the station's super had been too busy to do the filing today. As if he'd heard his thoughts, Denis called out from under the desk, "Can't find that bit of paper anywhere. Can't imagine where it's gone."

"What bit of paper?"

"Oh, something to do with you going to the university. Enrolment forms."

"News to me," said a mystified Ben.

"No-one said anything to you?"

"Not to my knowledge. But then I'm not very good at this telepathy thing."

"Hmm," came the quiet reply. "We'll have to tell them that. Anyway," added Denis, getting up and reaching over to the top of his filing cabinet, "here's your mission for today. Get Clarissa warmed up and both of you report back here. I'll have the necessary paperwork ready."

"What sort of mission is it?" Ben queried.

"Don't know yet. Call has only just come through. Apparently there has been discussion amongst the angels prompted by the results of your recent rescue. You and Malcolm have been chosen as just the right lads for this job. Best choice they said."

"Goodness!" exclaimed Ben, surprised that he and Malcolm had been the subject of such discussions.

"They were pleased with the way you handled everything." Denis raised an eyebrow as if he was surprised himself. "You might want to pack some gloves and a muffler, though. It's cold where you're going."

Ben reflected that he and Malcolm had just experienced cold. "Colder than the Alps?"

"Could be."

Ben took the hint and packed accordingly, also making sure that Clarissa's heater was working, just in case their brains did a double-take on all the white stuff. Imagination was a powerful thing.

They were flying high over some mountains. The scenery was breathtaking. "Denis must think we love this sort of weather. As an Aussie, do you mind?"

"Did a little skiing in Oz, up Mount Buller way."

"So that's a 'no' then?" remarked Ben.

"Snow. Lovely stuff," said Malcolm, leaning back in his seat as he mused about steep mountain slopes and snow-covered gum trees. He came out of his reverie. "Do you know where we're going? From Clarissa's orientation guide, looks like it's not home territory."

"Meaning?"

"Not the British Isles."

"Well, all I know is it's going to be cold. I've given Clarissa the co-ordinates according to Denis, so I'm hoping she'll take us to the right spot. It's certainly looking chillier out there and a storm has just started to blow. Or should I say a blizzard?"

"Hell, yes!"

Ben was about to say hell was not known for its blizzards, but decided against it. Malcolm peered through his side window, cupping his hands over his eyes, as if that would help them penetrate the gloom outside. It had suddenly become pitch dark.

A green light started to blink on Clarissa's dashboard. "We're getting nearer," said Ben. "Ok, Claris, let's start our descent whenever you're ready."

Her engine hummed in perfect harmony with her gears and she started to lose height. Outside the blizzard had lost none of its ferocity. "Good thing I thought to bring the goggles," Ben announced. "Maybe I picked up on somebody's good advice. This telepathy thing might be beginning to work after all."

"Lucky you," said Malcolm. "I don't think I'll ever get the hang of tuning into someone else's mind."

Ben was just about to reassure his partner it would come in time, when Clarissa braked hard and his mouth shut abruptly as both he and Malcolm lurched forward, seat belts straining against their shoulders. Clarissa steadied herself. They had landed on deep snow, but not one of her wheels had sunk even a millimetre into the white landscape.

Malcolm undid his seat belt, grateful for its security, and peered through the side window again. It was still snowing, though not as heavily. "How are we supposed to see anything in this?" he said.

"Well, I think we have to get out and explore. Perhaps, Clarissa, you could switch your lights to high beam? It might help for a while at least. Don't forget your torch, Mal."

Clarissa's lights shone far out into the night, illuminating a pathway for both men.

"See any movement?" Ben called as the two of them spread out, moving further and further away from the ambulance. Clarissa's headlights were becoming dimmer by the minute.

"Nope, not a sausage. Not even... Hang on, what's this?" Malcolm switched on his torch and bent down to the ground, picking up something red that immediately crumbled away in his hand. "Damn!" he muttered.

"What do you think it was?"

"Dunno. Long enough to have been a scarf, a flag, or perhaps someone's singlet? Hard to say."

"Must have been lying here for years."

"So, do you think we're looking for some crackpot explorer who's got lost? Got no time for them myself. Traipsing off into the unknown, causing mayhem for their rescuers."

"Causing mayhem? Explorers are no more crackpot than those idiots who fling themselves off the top of mountains, wearing a long elastic band strapped to their feet and hoping to stop before they reach the bottom!"

Malcolm grinned. "Yeah, great fun."

"Well, suppositions about our missing rescue case aren't helping us right now, and I'm beginning to feel uncomfortably cool, even though I know it's my imagination. How about you?"

"Back to Clarissa?"

They both nodded to each other and trekked back the way they'd come. There was only one problem. They couldn't find the ambulance. No lights illuminated the snow. There was just… nothing.

"Now where's she gone?" Ben was feeling exasperated at this unexpected turn of events. "Celestial ambulances don't just hike off into the distance and leave their drivers and attendants behind."

"Maybe she came to find us and got lost," Malcolm suggested, hopefully.

"No, she wouldn't do that. She's got far too much sense. She'd stay put, waiting for us to find her." Ben hoped he was right.

"No good waiting around, though," said Malcolm, hugging himself to keep warm. "Don't know about you but I'd rather keep moving than stand still."

Ben grunted in agreement, still perplexed at Clarissa's seeming dereliction of duty. Where was she?

They both moved off into the night, keeping close together. It had at least stopped snowing. As they trudged through the frozen landscape Ben began to wonder when Clarissa would take it into her head to turn up again. It was so damned cold! He tried to remember if the ambulance had a homing device that would pinpoint their position.

"Malcolm, can you remember what our last position was?"

"Somewhere around Baffin Island?" He pulled out his compass, but it wasn't proving to be much help. The compass needle was wobbling all over the place.

"And Clarissa," said Ben with a sigh, "bless her brake pads, has motored off with our map. I say let's keep moving. I can't stand this standing still, and at least we won't get frozen to the spot that way."

"Not possible is it, seeing as we're… well you know… departed souls?"

"I just know my mind is saying I'm feeling a lot blimmin' colder than is comfortable. Just an emotional reaction I suppose."

They set off at a brisk pace, with no other desire than to keep going, no matter where their feet led them. Their energy levels fortunately never diminished - the bonus of being in spirit as opposed to being physical – while up ahead the horizon was lightening, as if dawn was about to break. But it wasn't the sun coming up. It was Clarissa, shining her headlights in their direction.

"You wait `til I see her!" muttered Ben.

If it was possible for an ambulance to look apologetic, she made a good effort at it.

"Sorry guys, I got lost. Came looking for you after I got a message from Denis."

"What message would that be Claris?" asked Ben, barely concealing his impatience.

"It seems we were in the wrong place."

"You're joking!" he said, exasperated. "I didn't think Denis was capable of a slip-up of this kind."

"It wasn't his fault," muttered Clarissa.

"Whose then?"

"Did something change at the last minute?" asked Malcolm kindly.

Clarissa didn't answer straight away; she was sulking. She loved Ben, but she could see at the moment he didn't feel quite the same about her. "All Denis said at first was that the co-ordinates didn't make sense, and then a message got through after you'd left that we were in the wrong place, but it was too late to stop you. And then I tried to find you and got lost."

Clarissa's engine coughed and Ben could see she was upset. He was beginning to regret his hasty remarks. "Ok, luv," he said patting her bonnet affectionately, "let's get inside and we'll check your new co-ordinates."

It was while Ben was studying these, snug once more in a warm cabin, that he heard a voice calling to him from outside. He looked across at his partner to make sure he wasn't mistaken, but Malcolm just shrugged. He'd heard it too. Ben glanced through the side window.

The voice said again, "We need your help."

Ben opened his door to be met by a very tall Being. The fact that an icy wind cut the air like a knife had little effect on this person, who seemed to be clothed in nothing more than a rather handsome, but thin, robe. Politeness dictated that he and Malcolm step outside and greet their visitor. They both stared a long way up into a face that... well, made you feel surprisingly at peace within yourself.

"We knew you'd come," said the angel, who then added gently but firmly, "Follow me."

And they did, without question.

"Ben," said Malcolm, "I think we should assume this person we're following knows where to go."

"Wouldn't be anything to do with his being an angel would it?" quipped Ben.

"Yeah, I think you could safely bet on that. Do you think we could ask this one if he knows the other one we met on the mountain?"

Ben looked at Malcolm as if to say: *What do you think?*

"No, better not," considered Malcolm. "Must be thousands of them around."

"Well, when you think of the population of Earth at the present time, and that everyone has their own guardian angel... Of course, there's just a *chance* they have bumped into one another!"

The snow fell more gently now and the wind had eased. They walked in front of Clarissa, her headlights illuminating the gloom; and just as helpful was the light radiating from the angel.

"Come," they were urged. "We are nearly there."

Ahead they noticed a fairly human-looking lumpy mass in the snow, and standing beside it a very confused-looking soul. "The lost explorer?" said Malcolm.

"Dunno," replied Ben.

But the lost soul hadn't been an explorer. An airman instead - engine failed, radio out, 'plane down, nothing for it but to find help. He'd baled out, started walking and collapsed.

"Hello," said Ben. "Lost your way?"

He received a blank look. "What are you doing here?" said the airman.

"Rescuing you, mate," answered Malcolm.

"But it's too late. I'm dead aren't I, so it's too late." He looked unhappy about it.

"Not expecting life to go on," mouthed Ben to Malcolm, and then to the man, "Happens to a lot of people, sir. Don't worry, we're here to look after you."

The airman introduced himself as Harry. "Engine conked out," he said in a voice as sympathetic to his 'plane's fate as his own. "Knew I'd had it then, but when the radio went as well, I decided I'd rather die walking. I certainly didn't expect a welcoming committee. Do you do much of this?"

"We go wherever we're needed," Ben answered, taking the airman gently by the arm and steering him towards Clarissa.

"Yes, but how did you know where to find me?" Harry flung out an arm at the wide expanse of snowy, featureless landscape.

Ben hid a grin. "Let's say we had help," glancing at Harry's guardian angel.

"Oh, blimey," Harry gasped. "Wow, is that who I think...?"

"Yes, mate," affirmed Malcolm. "Now come on, sir, we need to get you seen to."

Harry allowed himself to be led back to an ambulance that he suddenly realised had materialised in the middle of a frozen nowhere. He soon gave up worrying about it once he'd been given a piping hot cup of tea and a warm blanket to wrap himself in.

Clarissa released her brakes and winged her way up through Earthly clouds, seamlessly entering the land that lay beyond the veils that separated physical reality from the eternal. Ben checked his wing mirror. A radiant, misty light was disappearing into the snowy distance.

Malcolm was in the back with Harry, chatting to him about harmless things that took his mind off his recent demise and encouraged him to think about the extremely nice place he was being taken to.

"What's it like there?" Harry asked.

"You'll see very soon," came the reply.

Harry was having none of it. "I want to know before we get there."

"We'll be there in a couple of secs. Anyway, it's a subjective thing. I can only give you my own impressions."

"Come on! Surely you can give me a clue?"

"Well, all I can say is that you'll feel you've come home. Any cares or worries will simply dissolve and you'll find yourself taking deep breaths of the freshest air you've ever tasted and feel the gentlest warmth you've ever felt... well, you'll just feel very much more alive than you ever did before."

"Wow, can't wait."

"Well, as I said, you won't have to, here we are now."

And it was true. Clarissa was her most gentle as she touched down outside the Lodge of Rest and Recuperation, delivering her latest patient into the care of the waiting Sisters.

Harry looked a little overawed at first, but then couldn't get the grin of pleasure off his face, smiling through his words as he said a "Thank you" to Ben and Malcolm, at the same time appreciating the sight of two lovely ladies who were ready to convey him into one of the wards.

Malcolm grinned as he watched Harry walking away, chatting to, or was it *up*, the nurses. "He's going to have no trouble fitting in!" he chuckled.

Later, on one of his regular visits, Ben asked how Harry was getting on. Apparently he had found his niche and become an almost indispensable resident.

"Once he was well again there was no stopping the silly boy," laughed Agnes. "He's the sort that can't sit still. Ants in his pants. But he's been a blessing, as long as we can control the speed he pushes the trolleys around the wards at."

Ben smiled. "I must get to see him sometime. Sounds the sort of feller we could do with at the station."

"Och, I don't know. We're a bit short-handed here. It would be a pity to lose him."

Ben now laughed out loud. "You, short-handed! I've never seen so many volunteers in one place."

"Ah well, but if they're anything like Harry it takes us all our time making sure they don't run away with themselves, causing more chaos than is here already! I must admit, though, that so far he's been very reliable, if a little too enthusiastic. At least he hasn't run the trolley over any nurse's toes!"

Back at the station, Ben and Malcolm were mulling over Harry's rescue.

"Another job well done, Mal. Time for a drink?"

"I won't if you don't mind. I'm meeting some friends. Haven't seen them for a long time… you know, want to catch up."

"Have a great time." And Mal disappeared with a puff of air.

Ben wondered if he should stay at the station. There was always something to do, even if it was just washing and polishing Clarissa. "I'm becoming boring. All work and no play," he muttered to himself.

Yes, but you have been so valuable in giving your time.

Ben looked around but couldn't see anyone who might be talking to him. "Horace, is that you?" No answer.

"Well, one day mister," he said to himself, "you are going to take a little more time off than usual and spend it catching up with your mates, and let work look after itself."

He could, of course, have decided right then and there to link into his friends, but after meeting angels he realised that all he wanted to do was be solitary, to reflect, and the Café Concertina was the perfect place. Although a busy rendezvous for many, it could also accommodate those who wanted to be solitary. Or those who thought they wanted to be solitary. He changed his mind at the last minute, with a sudden urge to sit amongst trees and flowers, on a comfortable garden bench.

CHAPTER 10

A Conversation With Rufus

In the Gardens of Remembrance there was always a place available for quiet reflection. It was at moments like this that Ben fully appreciated how blessed his life was compared with what it had been before. Earth had been a hard school, where he'd never felt he quite fitted into the scheme of things as he'd hoped; too many separate threads, and the difficulty of tying them together. Back then he had been a round peg in a square hole. Now, at Station One Two Zero he *did* fit in, loving the work he was doing and the people he worked with. Yet he instinctively knew there was something missing in his life.

Would *education* fill that hole? He glanced around, seeing vague, wispy shapes coming and going, then solidifying as form recognised the reality it inhabited, atoms and molecules adjusting to a different vibration. People bowed their heads to speak quietly with each other, bending down to talk to the children who joined their throng. Humanity was comfortable in these surroundings. This was, after all, the zone of comfort and love shared.

Ben became wistful, thinking of his Linda. She worked as a carer in an old people's home, a job she loved and was dedicated to. He was trying to picture her at her daily round, having a joke with her patients, listening to their stories, making them feel comfortable in what for some was an alien world; a step too far from what they had known until then. Her affinity with the elderly was, she had often reminded him, the reason she had decided to take the job. He knew that as a qualified nurse she could have taken work elsewhere, but the retirement home was where she felt happiest.

Ben wondered if she might appear in front of him now. Was it even night-time in England, when she would be dreaming? He knew it was possible for people to visit the gardens when they were asleep. He stared in front of him, waiting, just in case, and for a brief, shimmering moment he thought he saw her smiling face turned towards him, a hand lifted in recognition, and then she was gone. "Wishful thinking?" he asked himself.

He knew when he visited her, that Linda was able to sense his presence. She always turned her head when he came close, as if she had heard a door opening and was ready with a welcome. Sometimes she said his name out loud, confident he was there, though she could not have explained to anyone how she was so sure, only that she felt a warm glow deep in her heart, and then he'd be in her thoughts. It was at such times that it seemed as if he'd never gone away. He could be right there in her kitchen watching her cook a meal or doing the washing up, and she would share her day, keeping him up-to-date with the gossip.

"Susan's got herself into a bit of bother," she'd said last time, "calling in sick at work and then being discovered out and about shopping. Boss wasn't too pleased. It was a busy time for them at the office. Silly girl, she'll be lucky to keep her job!" Susan was the daughter of Linda's best friend, Pat.

"She'll make her apologies," assured Ben, "and hopefully the boss will forgive her. She's a good worker when all is said and done. And if she loses her job, well, she'll have learned a valuable lesson."

"She's young and inexperienced. Oh, dear," Linda sighed, "being young has its wonderful moments, but I wouldn't swap it for the experience you gain with maturity." She smiled then at where she thought he might be sitting comfortably at the kitchen table. He smiled back.

"I know you're there, you rascal. Dammit, but I wish I could *see* you!"

She touched her cheek as she felt his goodbye.

Ben so much wanted to continue to give Linda loving support. Horace had assured him that his visits did help, and that his brief glimpse of her in the gardens was a sign that she was gradually finding her way in her dreams. Sister Agnes had been a support, too. Since their first meeting he and the Sister had become good friends. Being of similar ancestry (he was still a child when his parents moved to London – they had never lost their accent, although he had), Ben found the Sister's soft Scottish voice made him feel he was with family. He was a new arrival compared to her, though he'd noticed she looked no older than he did; but then almost everyone here looked about the same age. It couldn't be denied, though, she had a maturity about her and an air that spoke of long experience in her field. If he was honest with himself he felt he didn't have any maturity at all. Agnes had taken him under her wing, understanding what it must be like for him being in that unfamiliar territory of loving someone who was far removed in more than just a physical way.

And then, as if thinking of her had sent out a signal, she was suddenly by his side, a hand on his shoulder as she greeted him.

"Hello, Ben."

"I was thinking about you, Sister."

"Maybe I needed to be here then. I've got some time off. Feel like a walk?"

"Sure."

"I saw Rufus the other day," Agnes remarked. "The lovely wee thing was doing his usual rounds and looking for someone to stroke his head, scratch his ears, make a fuss of him. Sometimes there's a gang of wee'uns following him, dogs and cats of all shapes and sizes, all out for a bit of fresh air, they tell me!"

"Sounds like Rufus is popular."

"Oh, yes, he's a fine little chap," she laughed. "And he tells me he's keeping an eye on you."

"Yes, well, I suppose he would say that," Ben laughed. "He always seems to know when I might be free to take some time off. We meet here. I meditate, Rufus sleeps with his tongue lolling out - says he's soaking up the light."

Agnes smiled. She knew how delightful that was.

As they walked they fell into a comfortable silence. It was only when Agnes stole a glance at Ben that she looked suddenly concerned.

"You're looking very thoughtful, Ben. Not your normal self?"

"I always look like this when I'm cogitating."

She laughed. "Sorry, that was a bit rude of me."

"You, rude? That'll be the day."

"Perhaps not," she agreed.

People passed and nodded a hello. Agnes found a bench to sit on, while Ben chose to lie at full stretch on the grass, letting out a contented sigh that didn't take long to get noticed. The air went plop by his ear, and in full white fluffiness Rufus materialised, panting expectantly for his ears to be scratched and, when they were, lifting his nose to the sky, meaning he wanted more of that, please. Agnes whispered to him that perhaps Ben could take him for a walk later, but Rufus thought back that his master was far too lazy for that, though he had already planned taking him on the long route back to the station.

Agnes giggled and Ben looked up at them both to see what was so funny.

"Rufus and I are having a private conversation, Ben. You shouldn't be listening in."

"I'm not, but your laughter woke me up. Not that I was really asleep. Don't seem to get tired like I used to."

"Well, there's no real need to sleep is there?" she said in her pert Scottish way. "Ah, but rest, that's different. We all like some time off now and again."

"How long have you been at the hospital, Sister?" Ben asked suddenly.

Agnes looked at him curiously. "Why do you need to know, Ben?"

"Just curious. I'm trying to find a pattern I suppose. I mean, do people decide how long they want to stay in one particular job, or do they have suggestions made, encouragement given, to move to something else?"

"You're wondering how long you'll be in the celestial ambulance service?"

"Yes, maybe. Don't get me wrong, I love the work, but I have a feeling there is something more – something extra - that I'll eventually find myself doing. And at the moment I don't even know why I'm thinking along those lines."

Agnes smiled and nodded to herself. "Well, there is the university calling you. That's your next step you could say." But after a pause, she felt she had to add: "Something inside of you knows, Ben, but I canna enlighten you about your path - I only know mine. I think everyone makes their own choices. Perhaps sometimes encouragement comes when it is needed."

Ben smiled at that.

"Don't rush to change things. Take me, for instance, I know that where I am, the work I am doing, is where I can be of most service, but I am alert to the possibility of that changing at some point. So far, however, no-one has nudged my elbow to say it's time to move on to something else."

Ben wondered what the 'something else' might be for anyone, not just him or Sister Agnes. But right now he felt too content to stretch his mind any further.

Agnes, it seemed, agreed, saying in a voice that showed she had never ever taken where she was for granted, "Don't you just love it here?"

Ben grinned up at her. "I do, Sister."

"Agnes is my name, Ben."

"Ok. Agnes."

"And now, Ben, I must leave you. I can hear Sister Martha calling. But don't you leave just yet. I believe Rufus has something to say to you."

Ben raised an eyebrow at his dog. "Well, Rufus, what is it?"

"Horace has asked me to pass on a message."

Ben was slightly taken aback. "Couldn't he come himself?"

"Well, he is going to, but I'm here first." Rufus looked at Ben, tilting his head to one side as if to say it really mattered that he said what he needed to.

"Ok, Rufus. I give in. Let me have it."

"You haven't filled in your enrolment forms for the university yet. Are you resisting, Ben? You know that education is good."

Ben looked down at his beloved dog. "Denis has mentioned enrolment forms, but I'm still not convinced that I'll be any good at all that learning stuff."

Secretly, Rufus knew how Ben had struggled at school. It wasn't because he wasn't bright or intelligent enough, he just didn't apply himself; no interest and no confidence, that was the problem.

"You have to do it," the dog barked. "Can't stand still. Education's good."

Ben looked at Rufus and shook his head. How could a dog know education was good? And where had he picked up such ideas? "But I like doing my ambulance job. That's enough for me."

Rufus was unfazed by Ben's comment. "Yes, you have your job and you're very good at it and it's important to keep it up. But eventually… well, it will become second nature to you again. You'll want another challenge."

Oh dear, the *challenge.*

"Will I?" said Ben, unconvinced.

"You'll still be able to do the rescue work and have time to do the studying. Clarissa would be upset anyway if you didn't turn up for work."

"Would she? Can an ambulance have feelings like that?"

"Well, normally they don't, but Clarissa's different," woofed Rufus, as if to confirm anything Clarissa did was guaranteed to be different.

"Yes, I've found that out," agreed Ben. "So this learning stuff, whatever it entails. You think I'll be ok at it?"

"Absolutely!" And to prove his point Rufus licked Ben's face all over, which was, he considered, the best encouragement he could possibly give his friend.

But there was no hurry, apparently, and for the moment they allowed themselves the contentment of just enjoying where they were. In the distance small groups of people and couples were walking around chatting or standing still for a moment and taking in the atmosphere of the place.

"This garden… it reminds me of something," said Ben.

"You used to come here when you were asleep - before you passed over. You came in your astral body."

"Did I? Never thought I went anywhere when I was asleep. Head on pillow and bang! That's me."

"Everyone comes here," Rufus continued. Ben smiled. It was good that they conversed telepathically, as he couldn't see how Rufus could say so many words with his tongue hanging the way it did, half out of his mouth. "You sometimes met your parents here."

"Well that begs the question why they aren't here to see me now!" exclaimed Ben.

"They're doing important work. They will be here as soon as they are able."

This was too much. In his mind Ben still thought of his parents as old people, too old to be working. "What work? And why do they need to work anyway?"

"Oh, it's very important work," Rufus replied. "But it takes them away from this dimension sometimes. They volunteered for it," the dog added, as if that settled the matter.

"Oh!" was all Ben could think to say in reply, but his brow creased into a deep furrow as he realised there was still such a lot he didn't understand about this new world. Would he ever stop feeling like a newcomer?

Rufus heard Ben's thoughts. "Only when you stop thinking you are."

Ben rubbed Rufus behind the ears, mulling over what he had said about his parents. "You say that I used to come here in my sleep. So, I could tell myself that this is all very familiar... and yet it isn't. I don't remember any of my visits, and if I did come here and saw my parents, shouldn't I have woken up afterwards feeling a sense of... well, some sense of being happy? I often woke up feeling miserable, which makes no sense if I'd just come back from such a beautiful place."

"Well, how did you view your life? Was it a painful life, or a beautiful one?"

"It was both. And it was very ordinary."

"So, perhaps sometimes when you woke up you were unhappy to be back in it."

"But that still makes it a pity that I didn't remember what I'd just left when I was asleep. I'm sure it would have helped to have remembered."

"No it wouldn't."

Ben was surprised. He looked at Rufus, his eyebrow raised in a silent question.

"What I mean is that you had to get on with your life, not go about living in a dream. If you had remembered where you'd been when you were asleep you would have done that – gone around in a dream instead of getting on with the uncool stuff of living an everyday life. Everybody loves it here. Sometimes it's difficult to get them to go back to their Earthly bodies because they love it so much."

Ben was imagining the reluctant ones digging their heels in and refusing to return to their everyday third-dimensional lives. He laughed. "How do you handle the recalcitrant ones? Bark them to distraction, so that they run screaming back to their beds?"

"Nooo. The Persuaders handle those who want to linger too long."

"The Persuaders? Sounds a bit pushy!"

"Sometimes pushy is the only way to get anyone to pay attention. But they're nice about it."

Ben smiled at Rufus, scratching him under the chin. He knew better than to pat his head and give him a headache, though he did wonder if headaches were possible where they were. Rufus certainly was an unusual dog. Who would have thought you could communicate with your pets so easily? He couldn't help thinking that on Earth certain pets *did* have a really good try at talking to their owners, but it must have been hard work.

He gazed around him at the beautiful scenery: the herbaceous borders that were always full of fresh, fragrant flowers that never wilted and trees that were not only always in bloom but also bore a never ending supply of fruit. Streams ran in and out of groves and copses, lawns always looked freshly mown. He took a deep breath of the fresh scent in the air, wondering lazily if those down on earth ever envisaged a place as wonderful as this. No, he was certain no-one could ever know quite what it was like unless they were here.

With Rufus's head leaning against his leg, Ben closed his eyes and leaned back, fitting snugly into the curved bench seat. There was a hint of the sweet flush of drowsiness.

Rufus may have had his head nodding, but he wasn't about to let himself fall into a deep slumber, even though the light was so warm and comforting and he had to blink his eyes a lot to stay awake. Someone was coming and he didn't want to be asleep when they arrived. For Ben, it was a case of hardly needing to open his eyes to know who was approaching.

"May I join you?" came the great resonance that was Horace's voice.

"Yes, of course!" replied Ben standing up to greet his friend. "It's always good to see you."

"I thought you might want some company, though I see that Rufus is quite capable of looking after you."

Rufus wagged his tail, which he did most of the time anyway, and grinned at their visitor. Horace stroked him all the way down from his head to his tail and then did it again. Rufus took the hint and lay down by Ben's feet and promptly went to sleep.

"You've been away! Busy?" asked Ben.

"Yes," replied Horace, giving no hint of what he'd been doing.

Ben wished he could have asked his friend what kept him so busy; not that he doubted his busyness, but it was a prick of curiosity that hadn't yet been satisfied, yet he felt he couldn't just ask outright. Horace might be involved in something he wouldn't understand anyway. Ben's mind drifted to all the unknown possibilities that might exist in this altered reality, where everything was a possibility just by thinking about it. Perhaps, he thought, Horace is involved with work that is too important and secret to discuss with anyone else, least of all me. He glanced at Horace to see whether he had picked up on his thoughts. Horace just gazed at the horizon ahead, his face calm and serene, undisturbed by questions that needed answers.

"Are you content, Ben?" he said at last.

"Why, yes, of course," Ben replied, suddenly thinking what a strange question to ask in a place such as this. "Why wouldn't I be?"

"But there is still a gap..."

"I've left someone behind. I think of her often. I visit her, to see how she's coping now she's on her own."

Horace nodded understandingly. "Linda. Yes."

"She knows when I'm around, but it all takes a bit of adjusting to, not being able to physically touch her, reassure her in that direct human way..." His voice trailed away.

"We do understand, Ben. In the wider scheme of things it is still early days for you. There are adjustments to be made for her and for you."

"Well, it's just that sometimes... you know, when I'm not working... I reflect a little..."

"You have also been thinking about your parents, wondering when you will see them. Rufus has said something to you about them?"

"Yes, he said they are busy people. I get the feeling I'm learning the lesson of patience."

"It's a virtue that many allow to pass them by."

Ben's eyes showed that he understood. "I *am* content, really content. I'm experiencing so many new things - amazing things - that part of me wishes I could return to Earth and tell everyone about it."

"You would only forget what it was you had to say."

"I think I'm still coming to terms with everything being so different."

"It's exciting for everyone, this new life, and rather like going on holiday for some. But for others adjustments have to be made. You settled in so quickly Ben, that perhaps this is just a delayed reaction from the reality of having left your old life behind. It will pass. Trust me."

"I do. I trust you a lot more than I trust myself."

"You like your job?"

"Oh, yes, I love it. At first I couldn't understand why I'd be back at an ambulance station, doing what I thought would be a repeat of something I'd done before and left behind, but it's very different, very different indeed. And to see these people we rescue coming out of the Lodge of Rest and Recuperation when they've recovered... well, it's just the best feeling."

"How would you describe being here, generally that is?" Horace asked.

"Well, most of all I feel blessed that I am *here* and not somewhere *else!*" exclaimed Ben.

Horace chuckled quietly. "It was a foregone conclusion where you would end up, Ben."

"Not to me. Didn't think I did anything special with my life to deserve all this."

"You had a good, kind heart. Everyone makes mistakes, it's how you learn, but your intention was always true to good values. That counts."

"Well, thanks. You know, what I really love about this place is the sense of freedom. Free to do everything you want to do, and do it well. And this telepathy thing, well that helps a lot, of course. It means you don't have to guess what people are really feeling because you get it straight away. There's no need to hide behind Earthly constraints, and no-one here has a selfish thought in their head, so you can never hurt another's feelings. That's so liberating."

"Yes, here there are no hidden agendas."

"Just love and trust."

"Ah, yes." Horace laid a hand on Ben's shoulder, as an encourage-ment. "Some time, Ben, when you are ready, I will take you on a visit. Somewhere special."

Just before he disappeared back into the ether from whence he'd come, Horace indicated to Ben that he should stay a little while longer. No explanation given.

And then, in the next fraction of a second, a shimmering image caught Ben's eye, and there they were. His parents. The three of them hugged and hugged until there were no more hugs to be had, and love poured out and into each of them. For a long time they just sat and felt the bliss of being in each other's company. But there were things to be shared, things to be said.

"I've been hearing how busy you are," commented Ben.

Sheila, his mother, smiled, a knowing hidden deep within. "Oh yes." And then she proceeded to tell how she and Terry, his Dad, felt so blessed to be doing such wonderful work.

"Which is?"

His Mum cast a quick glance at his Dad. What passed between them, Ben was sure, was a quick message of whether this was the right moment to tell him about it. It wasn't.

"Sorry, Ben," said his Mum. "But it's classified for the moment."

"It's ok. When the time is right." For Ben it was a disappointment, but also an understanding that there must be a good reason for things to be the way they were.

"But perhaps you can tell me how you found each other, when you passed over, I mean. I don't know how all of that works. Do you just know where the other one is? Or is it more complicated?"

"No, not complicated. It was easy," said Sheila, smiling. "Our energies recognised each other, so it was an immediate response, and we were just there... together, in the blink of an eye. Your Dad was waiting for me and he looked just the same. Now though, I'd think you'd agree we look younger, and fitter. Thank goodness."

Ben realised then they *were* just a little different from how he'd remembered them and with that thought they began to look even younger, more as they really were and should be.

Sheila kissed Ben on the cheek. His Dad gave him another big hug. "It's time for us to go, son. There's work to do. We'll catch up again soon, I'm sure of it. Anyway, welcome home!"

And before Ben could say anything more, they were gone just as quickly as they had come, melting into the ether.

Ben hummed happily to himself as he headed back to Station One Two Zero. The station was quiet and the noticeboard showed that all missions had crews out attending them.

"Nothing for me?" he asked Denis.

"Nope," replied Denis, noncommittally.

"Nothing at all?"

Denis looked up from his desk. "Well, not unless you can help me find your university enrolment forms. They seem to have gone missing. Can't find them anywhere."

"Don't worry about it. I'm certainly not. All in good time, eh?"

"Easy for you to say, but the university does like to be taken seriously. Anyway my lad, there's a message waiting for you."

"What message?"

"Look in your pigeon hole."

Ben was about to say, *but I just looked there and there was nothing*, when Denis added, "Just arrived this minute."

The note said to meet in the Café Concertina: signed, Sam.

"Take your time," called out Denis. "You never know with Sam how long he's going to be."

CHAPTER 11

The Orphanage Of St. Opheus

Ben waited for Sam with his eyes closed, listening to the hum of bumblebees in the sweet honeysuckle that clung to the wall of the café. A soft warmth filtered down from a gentle summer sky. *Bet he's gone to the Market Place instead.* Sam had a bad memory for locations.

"Hrmph," came the sound of someone trying to clear his throat, or perhaps trying to catch his attention. Ben opened his eyes lazily, just enough to give whoever it was standing in front of him the message that he didn't want to be disturbed.

It wouldn't do.

"Hello," said the stranger.

"Hello," replied Ben, finding himself being scrutinised by the startling figure of a man dressed in a bright emerald green suit (with tails), with orange hair, blue twinkly eyes and an orange moustache. Round his neck he wore a green scarf covered in white polka dots. Ben was sure this man bore a striking resemblance to a cartoon character in a comic, only not one he could precisely name at that moment.

"Um," Ben hesitated, "who are you?"

"I'm the man."

"The man?" Ben said as respectfully as he could to someone he'd only just met.

"Oh sorry, yes, of course, you wouldn't know. I get to meet so many people I always assume everyone knows who I am. Bit confusing isn't it, when you don't know who you're talking to and why they *are* actually talking to you?"

"Yes," said Ben with a tone of finality in his voice that said: *So why don't you just tell me who you are and stop waffling?*

"Now, then," said the man in a different voice. "That's enough of that, young lad." Ben realised he'd been able to read his thoughts.

"Sorry," he said. "Forgot, you see. Still some things I need to get used to."

"You're forgiven. Don't mention it."

Ben almost thought *I won't,* but stopped himself in time. "Thanks," he said instead. "So, who are you?"

"Sam. Sam the man. I spoke to you at the end of Denis's integrative communicator machine. He uses it for new recruits who haven't quite got the hang of the telepathic link."

"Oh, the telephone, of course! And it was you who arranged for me to meet Norman and go to that peace conference with his team. I *do* know who you are!" Ben said, smiling and putting out his hand to shake that of this strange person, who at that moment was standing with hands on his hips and a look in his eye that said: *Once met, never forgotten.* "It's nice to meet you at last, Sam. I got your message. So is this a social visit, or what?"

"More than a social visit," said Sam. "I'm thinking we should go on a little tour."

Ben brightened. Sam smiled.

"I'd really like that," said Ben.

"Good. I just need to let Denis know."

Sam blinked his eyes twice, closed them for a few seconds and then opened them with a look that said *Sorted.*

"They can have someone else to take your place if and when," he said. "So, no need to be concerned. Anyway I think Denis considers this is more important, and I would agree."

"How did you do that? You know, the telepathy thing. I'm fine about most things," said Ben, "doing the ambulance work and all that entails, but this thought transference thing... well, I haven't got enough confidence with it yet. People seem to contact me rather than me contacting them at the moment."

"Don't have to know how to do it. It just happens."

"Well, you looked as if you had to concentrate."

"Oh, that's just for show."

Ben grinned, appreciating the joke. "So, where're you taking me, if you don't mind my asking?"

"We're off to a very special place, back on Ground Zero."

"Earth you mean?"

"Yes. This is important for your education, my lad. You know about rescue missions, or at least the sort you're doing now, but what I'm going to show you is a somewhat different type of rescue mission. We won't be bringing anyone back with us for one thing! Anyway, I have had my instructions from Horace and he was quite specific about you doing this."

"Oh," was all Ben said.

"You *will* enjoy it, lad. Don't fret! We're going to visit a children's orphanage."

Ben couldn't imagine why Horace thought this was a good idea. Ben had never had much to do with children in his previous life or even, yet, in this one, so maybe it was a missing part of his experience that needed attention. He still couldn't quite see the point, though.

Sam enlightened him. "Part of what you will learn is that children are wonderful at understanding things that grown-ups spend a lifetime sorting out. As well as a few other things, like what you think you can't do but you really can." Sam gave him a wink that Ben thought must be a clue, but not one he could fathom. "You'll see," he added. "Now, firstly, we need an ambulance."

"I thought you said we weren't picking up..."

"Just for transport, laddie. Unless you have access to a Rolls Royce?"

"Well, I've often considered Clarissa might have been one of those at one time."

Sam chuckled. "Hmm, I know what you mean."

Back at the station, no-one seemed surprised at Sam's request, Barney especially. He nodded to Sam as if he'd known him for a long time. Barney was in charge of the maintenance side of things.

"I suppose you'll be wanting to take Clarissa, rather than any of the other ambulances?"

"Yes, Barney," replied Sam. "She will fit the bill splendidly."

"I'd feel more comfortable with her, Barney," Ben added. "Know what to expect."

"Well, they're all much the same you know, but if you insist, I don't see why not. When are you wanting to leave?"

Ben glanced back at Sam, who looked serious.

"That means immediately," nodded Barney, sagely.

Clarissa was looking her usual clean, white self.

"Hi, Claris. Mind if we hijack you for the day?"

"Not at all, Ben," she purred. "Engine is warmed up, and I'm ready whenever you are. Hello, Sam."

"Hello yourself, me beauty," Sam replied.

The ambulance blushed a delicate shade of pink, which enhanced the blackness of her tyres and the silver of her chrome. Ben patted her bonnet to calm her down and went to climb into the driver's seat.

"No need," said Sam. "I'll drive. Easier than trying to direct you when you don't know where we're going."

"Can't Clarissa plan the route?"

"This is a surprise. So, no, not even Clarissa knows where we're going. But I can tell you it won't be familiar home territory for you."

"Not in the UK, you mean?"

"That's right. A place so remote, its people still haven't caught up with the twenty-first century."

"And we're going to do what?"

"We are going to keep faith with them. It's one way we can help. Haven't you ever had the experience of something fortuitous happening in your life, something unexpected?"

"You mean serendipity?"

"Yes, something like that. Well, where do you think that comes from? How does that happen?"

"Never considered it enough to think about it. Just called it luck."

"Mmm, I think many people call it luck. Where we're going is a place that needs plenty of that, as do the people we are going to meet. Anyway, my lad, you'll see soon enough. Now buckle up!"

Sam undid the buttons of his jacket so that he could sit more comfortably and removed his spotted green scarf, placing it neatly in the glove box. Then he smoothed his hands over his hair before locking them around the steering wheel. "Here we go," he sang in a bright, breezy tenor voice. Clarissa's dashboard lit up, she honked her horn and her engine purred into a higher rev.

They cruised over the countryside and then out over the sea. Ben had no idea where they were going; it was an adventure, and he was perfectly at ease because he knew he was in safe hands, even though he knew next to nothing about the person he was with. But then Sam was one of those people who had the happy knack of making you feel looked after when he was in charge.

They were cruising over land again and starting to lose height. "Where are we?" asked Ben.

"Just coming down to land. And in answer to your question, you just need to know we're somewhere!"

They were passing over a few sparse buildings, a farm or two, narrow country roads, and then up ahead a large rambling house. "That's where we're going," said Sam, pointing a finger. "It's an orphanage, and I think you'll find it interesting."

As Clarissa's tyres gently touched down, Ben unbuckled his seat belt and looked across at his companion. "I'll follow you."

"Okey-dokey," came the cheery reply. "Don't forget, the adults won't see us, but you can bet the children will. Clarissa, my beauty, you can relax your hubcaps and park yourself where you won't get in the way. Not that anyone will notice you, but it doesn't do to have people upsetting their metabolism by walking through you and having shivers running up and down their spines."

"Ok, Sam," Clarissa said in a sultry voice. "Anything you say."

Ben raised an eyebrow.

Inside the orphanage of St. Opheus there was pandemonium. Staff were rushing about everywhere in a flurry of activity, some carrying pails of water, others armfuls of towels.

"It's bath time," commented Sam. "The girls aren't so bad, but the boys hate it."

Ben understood. There was a certain age when boys thought it was definitely not cool to be clean.

"They need a firm hand then?"

"Oh yes, the Sisters here have their hands full. They're a great bunch though. Forget what you've heard about some orphanages in far off places. This one is wonderful, but they have too many children for the accommodation that's available and most of the staff are tired out much of the time. That's where you and I come in."

"Oh," said Ben, not quite understanding how he and Sam could make things any easier.

"Follow me," said Sam.

They went through the lobby, down a long, gloomy corridor. Ben noticed the paint on the walls was peeling off at an alarming rate, large flakes lying abandoned on the floor. "They don't get help clearing this up?" he queried.

"No, they don't get any help."

They turned right at the end of the corridor and Ben found himself in a small room with a large desk. Behind it sat a woman, her grey hair caught up negligently in a knot at the top of her head, loose strands trailing down her neck.

"This is Matron Agatha," whispered Sam.

"Why are we whispering?" asked Ben.

"Don't know," Sam shrugged. "But I always do when I come here. Out of respect I suppose."

Ben watched as Sam went round the desk and stood close to Agatha. Very gently he laid his hands on both her shoulders. She straightened her back and began to sit more firmly back into her chair. A small sigh escaped her lips and she closed her eyes. Sam kept his hands where they were and very gradually a whisper of light began to descend on to her head, floating down through her body, all the way to her fingertips and her toes. Although she was still sitting very upright Ben could see how much Agatha had now relaxed, and a gentle smile began to light up her face; whereas before it had looked so grey and sorrowful, now it looked calm and at peace, even quite attractive.

"That's better, me dear," said Sam, taking his hands away and leaving Matron sitting quietly at her desk. He motioned to Ben to follow him. "She'll be up and about again in a few minutes, but she'll feel like she's had a good two hours sleep."

"How do you do that?"

"Practice my lad. Just practice."

They moved on through the orphanage. Everywhere was chaos, the children full of high jinks and naughtiness - that is, until Sam entered the room. Then suddenly it seemed they were trying to behave themselves.

"They know who you are, then?" said Ben.

"Oh yes, they know who I am. They feel my presence. Children are amazingly receptive, you know, to things unseen by others. They're also my little darlings and they know that, too. They can be cheeky, even when I'm around, but they know I don't stand any nonsense with their behaviour as far as the staff is concerned. They have to learn to respect those who are helping them and it's never too early, in my experience, for children to learn that."

It was true, the children were managing to quieten down a little. They were still full of high spirits and Ben could see they were very much loved; but what an almost impossible task – hundreds of orphans and so few staff.

Before they were a quarter of the way round, Ben had stepped in to help. He followed Sam's lead and went where he was directed, making contact as Sam had done with Agatha, bringing in the ray of light that lightened the staff's load, easing their tired minds and bodies; and then with the children, calming their high spirits for a few minutes at least. The ray was called *Hope*, and it brought with it the knowledge that out there somewhere someone knew of the good work that was being done and cared about it.

"Is there any way we can get them some practical help? I mean from the outside community?" Ben was looking at the paint litter in the corridors.

"Good idea," nodded Sam. "I've attempted to do it on my own before, but perhaps with both of us..." Sam's voice trailed off, his focus for a moment somewhere else, somewhere distant. His head bobbed once or twice, as if a point had been made that he agreed with. Finally, he pursed his lips and said to Ben in a determined way, "Perhaps it's worth a try."

Ben had no idea what he meant.

The nearest town was about five kilometres away. They decided the local inn was probably a good place to start.

"Ok, Ben, what do you suggest we do?"

"Gosh, Sam, I thought you would be the one with the bright ideas."

"Well, seeing as you thought of this, I reckon I can trust you to make the right decision yourself."

Ben thought for a moment, hoping for some inspiration, and then his gaze fell on a man sitting in a corner, away from the bar, next to a window. His clothes were the shabby side of neat and looked as though he'd given them a good few years to get that way. He seemed to be brooding over a problem, elbows on the table, chin cupped in his hands and a tell-tale deep line etched across his brow.

"You can tune into his thoughts," suggested Sam.

Ben wasn't sure he'd be any good at this, but Sam nodded as if to say, *Give it a go. Nothing to lose.*

It didn't take long. The man's thoughts came over loud and clear into Ben's mind: *I've lost my job, what am I going to do? Can't tell the wife, or the kids. What hope is there for us?*

Ben looked at Sam forlornly, shrugging his shoulders. He couldn't see how he could help the man, let alone see him helping the orphanage. Sam stared back at him: *Don't give up. Use the ray.*

Ben laid his hands on the man's shoulders and allowed the ray of Hope to pour through. Instantly the man's brow cleared. He finished the half-empty glass in front of him in one gulp, stood up and walked out to the street.

"Blimey, that was a bit quick," said Ben. "What happened?"

"Beginner's luck, I presume," chuckled Sam. "You lifted the cloud of confusion that was preventing him seeing what he had to do. Let's follow him, shall we?"

The man had a bicycle parked outside. He climbed on and began to pedal furiously away from the town. Ben and Sam followed, gliding effortlessly behind the man, who was beginning to build up quite a sweat.

"Exciting," whispered Sam to Ben. "And I think I know where we're headed."

CHAPTER 12

Where There's A Will...

At St. Opheus, the man parked his bicycle and knocked on the large wooden front door. The knocker was a heavy, iron thing, wrought in the days of wealth and prosperity.

A female face appeared around the door. "Yes?" It was one of the Sisters.

"Hello, Sister, can I speak to Matron, please?"

"Yes, of course. Do come in."

They both walked down the same corridor that Ben and Sam had taken not one hour ago, turning right at the end and into Matron's office. Agatha looked up from her paperwork. She smiled pleasantly at the man.

"Hello, Jon. What can I do for you?"

"Well, Matron, it's more a case of what I can do for *you*, in return for what you can do for me."

"Sorry, Jon, I'm not following you. Can you be more explicit?"

"Yes, of course. It's like this, see, I need a job, and..." The man looked down at his shuffling feet, trying to concentrate on standing still and yet thinking about how he was going to say what had to be said. "I'd like to come and work for you. You know, do some handyman jobs, that sort of thing."

"Oh, Jon, that would be wonderful. But there is a small problem. We don't have any money to pay you."

"Well, Matron, I've thought about that. The mayor owns the largest hardware store in town and I thought that perhaps with a little encouragement he just might let us have some paint. For free!"

Matron Agatha smiled, almost chuckled, but it was not a smile of confidence, more a smile of pity. "And what makes you think Mayor Smelzer would be the least bit interested in the orphanage, or even in giving us some paint? And anyway who is going to pay you?"

"I don't know Matron. I just got it in my head that it was worth asking him for a favour. Perhaps it's a silly idea after all, but if you don't try you don't get, if you get my drift. I've never spoken to the mayor before, but then he *might* be someone who cares. Who can tell whether a person cares or not, if you don't get to know them? And I would have thought that as the orphanage is in his jurisdiction, he *should* care, shouldn't he?"

"Ah, there's the rub, Jon. Not everyone thinks like you. Not everyone cares about what is happening at the end of their street, or even next door, so how can we assume the mayor will care about an orphanage that is five kilometres out of town?"

Jon mumbled into his chest, "I don't know." Poor Jon, it looked like his bright idea was falling on barren ground, a seed that would wither and die before any drop of rain could nourish it into life.

Suddenly, Matron Agatha stood up. "You're right, Jon. If we don't try we don't get, and I've thought of something that might, just might, help the mayor make the right decision. How about we both go into town together in my rickety old van and front up to him, just ask him outright, will he help or not? Just like you did with me. The worst that can happen is he'll say 'No', and the very best is that he'll say 'Yes', or even, 'I'll think about it!'"

Jon's face lit up. "Yes, Matron, that's a great idea. Let's do it. Let's do it now!"

And so they got into Agatha's van, with Ben and Sam hitching a lift in the back. The van certainly was rickety and bumped over ruts and potholes in a lopsided, swinging motion that meant Matron Agatha had to keep a firm hand on the steering wheel and never take her eyes off the road. Jon decided it was best not to distract her with idle conversation.

They pulled up outside the mayor's office. Agatha applied the handbrake as they were parked on a slight slope, and put the car into first gear just in case.

"Well, Jon, here goes," she said as they marched up the two steps in front of the small but smart stone building in the town square.

She rang the bell on the front door, not once but twice. It was cold standing outside, a stiff breeze had started to blow and Agatha was wishing she had put on her warm coat instead of hastily picking up her knitted wrap. Jon was still warm from his cycling and sweating from a bad case of nerves.

The large, heavy wooden door creaked open. Agatha thought to herself that it wouldn't hurt to oil the hinges, or perhaps this door wasn't opened enough to warrant looking after the hinges.

"Good day," she said pleasantly. "We've come to see the mayor."

"Do you have an appointment?" said the clerk, an austere-looking fellow in a high white collar and black suit. Matron Agatha was firm and not a bit put out by this frosty reception.

"No, we don't. We haven't time to make appointments. This is urgent." And with that she pushed the door open wider and, with Jon following in her wake, strode straight towards the door with gold lettering on it, saying *Mayor's Office*.

"You can't do that," said the clerk in a thin, quavering voice.

"Well, I am doing it," Agatha replied, knocking firmly on the door.

"Come in," came a voice from inside; it was a big, burly voice, but Agatha wasn't the least put off. She had the bit (as the saying goes) firmly between her teeth and she was ready for anything. Sam and Ben kept close to her, Sam especially. Ben could see Sam's aura and Matron's were almost touching, their colours vibrant, harmonising.

Agatha's confidence was on a high.

"Hello, Mayor Smelzer. I've come with a proposition."

The mayor looked up, his eyes wide with disbelief. What a cheek this woman had, coming in unannounced and without even making an appointment! The clerk stood in the background, flapping his hands helplessly, his face a picture of dismay that the mayor had been interrupted and himself bamboozled by this woman.

"It's all right, Karl," said the mayor. "You can return to your office. I'll handle this."

Agatha, not in the least put off by the less than warm reception, continued almost without taking a breath. "My proposition is one that I think will be of as much benefit to you as to myself, and also to Jon here."

Mayor Smelzer looked at the determined woman standing in front of his desk, a small muscle beginning to twitch beneath his right eye. To anyone in the know this would have been a signal for danger, but either Agatha accidentally didn't notice, or deliberately didn't notice.

"And what could that possibly be, Matron? A loan perhaps? You people are all the same, wanting money and free handouts."

"Not this time, Mayor. All we want is to propose a business opportunity for you."

The mayor laughed out loud. "What sort of business opportunity? I've got a thriving business already. Why should you of all people think that you could offer me anything more?"

"Well, I'd like to offer you a chance to broaden your business base. You only service the locals, don't you? Perhaps you could look wider afield, service customers from the city, for instance."

The mayor grunted in a huffy sort of way. Here was this woman, this old woman (to him she was old, but to everyone else she was ageless), telling him she could help his business. Her impertinence knew no bounds. Nevertheless his eyes had begun to gleam at the suggestion she'd made. Perhaps he should hear her out after all? City customers - now there was a thought! The mayor liked being a big fish in a small pond, but even better was being a big fish in a big pond. However, he wasn't sure that anything the Matron suggested could possibly make this come true.

"With the greatest respect, Matron, there's nothing you could suggest to me that could possibly be of interest."

Ben couldn't stand people who said 'with the greatest respect'. Why couldn't people just be honest, in a kind way, and say what they really meant, like: *Sorry, but what you're offering is not what I'm looking for, but it was nice of you to think of it.*

Agatha was speaking again. "Oh, but Mayor, I think this would be a wonderful opportunity for you. I'm sure we could work together on what I have in mind. I can see your advertisement in the local paper being placed right alongside the article that tells everyone just how generous you've been in donating enough paint to completely redecorate the whole of the orphanage, and in addition how you paid for a handyman to do the job. Just think of the plaudits you will receive. The whole city will like you and they'll flock to your store and buy even more of your hardware, because they'll think of you as a kindly person worthy of their custom."

The mayor wasn't completely convinced by this argument. Give away free paint? It was a ludicrous idea. For the moment, he'd mentally blanked out paying for the handyman.

Sam was now standing behind the mayor, indicating to Ben to stand close to the Matron, though Ben didn't think Matron Agatha needed any help from him. However, he did as he was asked and watched as Sam laid his hands on the mayor's shoulders and very gently, but firmly, sank his fingers into tense, rigid muscles, soothing away the anger and replacing it with a deep peace. Sam could read the mayor's thoughts and buried deep within... ah, here was a sadness, a deep sadness that had made him mistrust the world and everybody and everything around him.

Many years ago, as a young boy, the mayor and his mother had been turned out of their family home. They hadn't been able to pay the rent and the bailiffs had come and taken everything away - all their possessions, even a wooden toy that his father had made for him, his only toy. His mother had pleaded with the bailiffs that her husband would return soon. He was away working on a very well-paid job. Money took a long time to travel back to them. They were sure it was coming.

The bailiffs and the landlord hadn't cared and so it was that a young boy and his mother had landed on the street, homeless. A good neighbour took them in and Tomas Smelzer had had to get a job. He was only twelve years old. His education suffered and for this and for everything that had happened at that time he bore a grudge. Throughout the following years the grudge had grown into a monstrous, gnawing hate. Now, at last, he was the one with power and he revelled in being safe and secure in that power. Now *he* was the one who didn't care.

Sam poured more light and hope into the mayor's mind and body. It was difficult, removing the mistrust built up over the years and the mayor resisted. But not for long.

Suddenly he looked up from the papers on his desk and straight into Matron Agatha's eyes. "Perhaps we can discuss this further," he said. "Would you like to come back tomorrow?"

"Yes, Mayor, yes, that would be fine with me. And I'll bring Jon, too?"

"Yes. Do come, too, Jon," said the mayor.

And so it was settled. Matron Agatha went ahead with her plan to bring in a reporter from the local newspaper, while the mayor organised his own advertisement. A half-page one would do, he felt, as long as it was next to the reporter's article.

Matron had also suggested that another reporter, from a city newspaper, might be contacted. "Newspapers are very good at spreading good news as well as bad," had been her observation. "Sometimes they prefer to print the bad news, but I've noticed that when the news is good, more people read it, rather than skim over the headlines."

The mayor had looked nervous when mention was made about the city newspaper. Everything was happening so quickly, he felt he was losing the plot, though it was clear Matron Agatha was not. He needed more time, he had pleaded with her. But it hadn't worked. And what was going to happen, he speculated to himself, if news of his good works (which hadn't happened yet) were broadcast not just locally but to folks in the big city? Matron's implication that he would become famous as a benefactor worried him a great deal. He didn't want to be giving money out left, right and centre to anyone who decided they wanted free paint or the wages for a handyman. She had some front, that Matron, asking for him to pay Jon's wages as well.

He sat back in his comfortable leather armchair, by his comfortable open fire, the logs hissing and spitting as the resin caught the flames, mirroring a little of what he felt in the pit of his stomach. "Perhaps," he thought to himself, "I could just do this one job, supply some paint, pay Jon for his work, and then when it's all finished I can get back to my business and think no more about the orphanage. I can afford to do this one little thing." And with that he sighed contentedly and slipped into a light slumber.

Meanwhile, Matron Agatha was laying her plans. She knew, really knew, that once the newspapers got hold of the story the mayor would find it difficult to resist giving them further help and even – bless the Lord – perhaps helping other worthy causes. "He's a good man at heart, I know," she said to herself. And to Jon she said, "I think we'll be doing the mayor a good turn. I think he'll want to be more involved with the orphanage in future. You'll see. And I think we'll be wanting to keep you on."

Jon's face broke out into a broad grin. "There's no stopping you, Matron."

"No, Jon, there's no stopping me."

Sam looked across at Ben as they both buckled up their seat belts. "Well, Ben, that's a good day's work done."

"Whew, I'd say. You know, Sam, I'm really glad you came to see me. I wouldn't have missed that for the world. I see that part of what I needed to learn was confidence in myself and how there are so many different ways of helping people, and not just those who have passed over to the Summerland."

"Perhaps at some later time you'll have the opportunity to see more ways we can help."

"Do you think the mayor's qualms can be overcome or resolved, you know, about being a general open purse for anyone who has a mind to ask for financial help?"

"I'm sure Matron will organise everything to suit the mayor's needs as well as those of deserving cases. She has a strong work ethic that won't allow hangers-on to abuse any good intentions the mayor might have. I can see them benefiting in many ways from their shared experiences. He will, I foresee, become more successful in his business *and* happier than he has ever been. The children will adore him, as will the staff. And as for Matron Agatha... well, they will become the firmest of friends."

"And maybe a little more?" suggested Ben.

"Maybe," replied Sam. "That's up to them."

Ben smiled deeply within himself, grateful that such wonderful outcomes were possible. Out of struggle could come laughter and happiness. In his mind's eye he was picturing the mayor surrounded by giggling and excited children, eager for his attention, eager for him to join them in a game or pleading with him to tell a story. The mayor considered himself a good storyteller.

"Yes," said Sam, tuning into the picture in Ben's mind, "it will be just like that, and there are plenty more similar stories that are yet to happen, even if you may not have the chance to see them all. You've got your own work to do, haven't you? And I mustn't keep you away from that too long. I think Clarissa would like to get back to the work she knows, too."

Clarissa nodded her approval of Sam's words by flashing her dashboard lights and honking her horn.

"But I'll have a chance to do some more work with you, won't I?"

"We'll see, Ben. We'll see. You'll need to check with Horace. I'm sure he's got many other experiences lined up for you. For now, let's just get you and Clarissa back to base."

CHAPTER 13

Justin

They descended in a leisurely way. Station One Two Zero looked peaceful and orderly. Sam was in a hurry and said he had things to do elsewhere, firstly to report back to Horace. Just before he disappeared he called over his shoulder, "Sister Agnes will be contacting you soon." And then he was gone, spotted green scarf and all.

Ben looked puzzled. "I wonder what she wants to see *me* about?"

"Don't know," chimed Clarissa. "Probably not urgent, though, or she'd be here to meet you." Her windscreen wipers gave a swipe as if to confirm that it was nothing to do with her.

"Hmm. Maybe I'll call in at the hospital and check."

"Good idea," she said breezily. "And while you're gone I'll get Frank to look at my spark plugs. I think I need a tune-up. We've been so busy lately."

Ben chuckled to himself. He knew Clarissa had no need for spark plugs, but she always liked to be in tip-top condition. Once again he wondered if she'd once been a Rolls Royce in another incarnation. "You just want an excuse to get rid of me, madam!"

"Not at all," she quipped in a haughty manner.

A light was flashing on her dashboard. "What's that, Claris?"

"It's a message coming through from Denis." On her screen words were appearing in a desultory way. "He really should practise his keyboard skills. He says he needs to see you right away. Urgently!"

"Why am I so popular all of a sudden?"

"Beats me. Anyway, he's waiting for you in his office."

But when Ben got there the office was empty. He ran his fingers through his hair, wondering what to do next, when a pile of files on the desk began cascading one-by-one onto the floor. Bending down and scrambling to catch them, he banged his head not against the desk but against something almost as hard.

"What the...?"

"Sorry, Ben," said Denis. "I thought I'd get back sooner rather than later. Thought the files were in a steady pile, too. How wrong can you be?" He grimaced, rubbing a sore spot on his head.

"How did you do that?" gasped Ben. "You weren't here and then you were."

"Oh, it doesn't take much practice."

"I know, everything is just a thought away. Boy, you did give me a start, though."

"Anyway," said Denis, still rubbing his head, "you'll be glad to know I found your papers. I put them in a safe place. Now, where was that..?"

"What papers?"

"Enrolment forms. For the university."

"Oh, I'd forgotten about them."

"Hmm, well I hadn't. Not allowed to, apparently."

"Do I really have to do this academic stuff?"

"We all do at some time or other. Now, where are they? Just like them to walk off, knowing you've no interest." Only one of those accusations was true. "By the way, how did it go with Sam?"

"Great! Wonderful experience. Does Sam do much of that sort of thing?"

"All the time." The station super breathed out heavily. But maybe the sigh was more to do with frustration as he continued rifling through the files on his desk; those that *were* at least still on his desk and not on the floor. "I think most people feel Sam has a special knack for understanding what needs to be done. And he does love to help people. He's quite a character isn't he?"

"Yeah. I learned a lot, especially that there's a good heart in every-one. It just needs some encouragement to show it."

Denis was now at the filing cabinet, still searching for the elusive en-rolment forms. He heaved another sigh and scratched an ear as if that would help stir his memory. "Sorry, Ben, I've mislaid them again. Well, it seems that the university is on hold for a bit longer. Look, there's no need for you to hang about here. We've two crews out and the rest are on standby, so why don't you go and see your mates, or whatever it is you boys get up to when you're not here."

"Hmm," pondered Ben. "Somehow I think they're all spoken for."

"Tuning in are you?"

"Takes practice!"

Denis grinned. "Good lad! Well, how about you start practising some time off. Right now!"

"Ok, ok, I'm going. Anyway I need to see Sister Agnes. Perhaps this might be a good time."

"Hmm," grunted Denis, already back at his filing cabinet.

Sister Agnes was waiting in her office, smiling as she looked up from her desk. "I thought you'd be here soon. I've had enough of paperwork. How do you feel about a walk? Your dog can come too." Ben glanced down at his canine friend, who had just then appeared out of the ether, sitting on his haunches as if it was his firm intention to stay.

"You don't want to join us, Rufus?"

"I would, but I feel I'm meant to be here to make a visit."

At that moment one of the nurses came by. "Rufus, there's an old lady who arrived recently. Would you mind showing her animal com-panion how to find Ward IVB?"

"Is this something you do on a voluntary basis?" asked Ben, trying to hide a broad grin.

"When I'm asked," the Westie replied with dignity.

"So is it a dog thing?"

"It's a cat this time," said the nurse.

Ben gave Rufus a look that said: *And you're ok with that? You never liked cats before.*

"I'm ok with it," came the stoic reply. And with that he strode off, tail in the air, heading for Ward IVB. On the way a feline figure, tortoiseshell, coalesced out of the ether and rubbed herself against Rufus's white fur. "That'll do, madam," he said to her, crisply.

Ben and Agnes took a table by the honeysuckle at the Café Concertina. Ben hummed a tune he suddenly couldn't get out of his head and waited for his drink to cool. He always ordered it too hot. Agnes twirled her cup round and round on the saucer.

"Aren't you going to drink that?" Ben asked, interrupting his humming mid-phrase.

"I don't know why I thought it up. Don't need it really."

"I know you don't but it would be a pity not to have it, all that good thought-form going to waste."

Agnes looked at Ben and seemed about to say something, but then hesitated and glanced instead down at her cup again.

"Something on your mind?" Ben asked gently.

She smiled ruefully. "Ben, I've a confession to make. I wanted you to come because I have a favour to ask of you. There's someone I'd like you to meet. I knew as soon as I saw him you'd be just the right person to help."

Ben wasn't fooled by Agnes's bright tone of voice. "Hang on, more information please! Who is this someone and why are you asking *me* to help him?"

"A new arrival," the Sister continued, unabashed. "I thought you could take him under your wing. He needs a little grounding and understanding of certain responsibilities. He's not sure what he wants to do now he's here. He's a bit cheeky, but bright, and if he can get away with doing almost nothing I have a feeling he will."

"A likely lad who soon gets bored?"

"A lot of youngsters are like that."

"Does he think everything's a free ride?"

"I don't know him well enough for that. I thought as you and Clarissa are such a good team and you're available right now..."

"But I'm meant to be taking some time off!" Ben spluttered in mid-sip, spilling tea. There was no stain on his jacket, the tea had just dissolved into the ether as soon as it left the cup. Sister Agatha, however, was in full swing.

"... that perhaps the both of you wouldn't mind taking him on a wee mission with you. It will help put things into perspective for him, open his eyes to what we really have to deal with. You might even get him interested in doing ambulance work."

"Has he had any training yet?" Ben asked cautiously.

"A little. He's a bright lad. He'll pick everything up, I'm sure of it."

Ben sighed the sigh of someone who knows he's been manoeuvred into a tight corner and can't make an excuse to get out of it. "Sister, as it's you I'll give it a go. But first we need to check with Clarissa, how she feels about it. She's having a tune-up right now anyway."

"Oh, that's all sorted. She's ready and waiting."

"And not complaining?"

"Weeell…" Agnes said in a long drawn-out sigh, "she'll do it, as long as you're driving. She tells me these youngsters love a joy ride, and without the fear of hurting themselves they like it too much." She looked at Ben again, soft blue eyes twinkling. "So, you'll do it? You'll do it for me?"

Ben sat up, as if that clinched the deal. "For you, Sister, I'd do anything."

"Remember, Justin is just a lad with little life experience. He's lovely under all the bravado - just a little too much for some people to cope with."

Ben smiled, but inwardly groaned. He'd already accepted.

Justin had been just eighteen years old when he'd been knocked off his motorcycle on the A303, near Wincanton in Somerset. He hadn't suffered. The suddenness of his death, together with the shock to his astral body, meant he flew out of his physical body almost before the impact. There's that few seconds before an event happens when you know you are heading in the wrong direction if you want to stay alive. That was how it was for Justin.

Justin had had no trouble adapting to his new life on the Other Side. A mischievous character at heart, he had a tendency to look at life as one big opportunity to have fun. His light-hearted pranks, however, did not, to his surprise, prove to be as funny as he had hoped, added to which the end result usually rebounded on him with incredible accuracy and speed. But he could always see the joke, and nobody's self-esteem was any the worse for the experience.

Mindful of Justin's track record, Ben decided that he would not be putting him behind the driver's wheel on his first day out, which of course led to disappointment for Justin and a smile from Clarissa.

"I had to sit in the attendant's seat on my first day and it's better that way," Ben said, implying that was an end to the matter. "You'll get your chance, but not yet. Anyway you're too keyed up, like a spring ready to burst its coil. You've got to calm down a bit before you can take the wheel."

"I'm only excited because this is my first time, boss."

"I'm not your boss, Justin, and I will tell you when you're ready to drive this vehicle." Ben was firm. He treated youngsters sympathetically, without ever being patronising. He knew they would learn.

"Ok, chief," said Justin cheerfully. "Whatever you say."

"I'm not your chief either. Got it?"

"Yes, sir."

Ben decided this was just going to be one of those days and there was no point in continuing what he knew would be a tit-for-tat conversation with this bright young lad. Anyway, he was beginning to think he might like Justin. He just needed to lose some of his brashness. Today there were no emergencies, so it was a good opportunity to get to know the lad, who at the moment was fidgeting with his seat belt.

"You'd better buckle that up in a hurry. It's there for a reason."

"Why do you need them over here anyway?"

"Over here may seem safe most of the time, but sitting in an ambulance called Clarissa is an unknown quantity. The fact is she likes to brake at the last minute, hard! And she never gives you any warning."

Justin looked as if he found this hard to believe.

"I'm not joking."

"Right, I get it." Justin hastily buckled up.

Ben looked out of the window at the passing landscape below. The sun shone with crystal brightness, the sky a bewitching shade of opal blue. A surge of complete satisfaction filled his soul as they soared above rolling hills and green valleys, rivers sparkling in the distance and a slight haze lolling about the meadows. He had not a care in the world and flew as if he owned the sky. Clarissa, too, was enjoying the freedom of this moment, to go anywhere she liked, with no fixed destination in sight. She flew steadily and true, humming a little tune to herself.

"What's that, Claris?"

"Don't know the title, but it's one I picked up from the radio. Can't get it out of my head. It's catchy isn't it?"

He wasn't about to argue with her, even though Clarissa's version of humming was more a burst of irregular engine noises.

"Yes, very catchy Claris, but I think we need to be quiet for the moment. I need to check in with Denis. He said something earlier about keeping in touch."

"Oh, ok," she sparkled, still feeling upbeat about her humming.

Justin looked at Ben with an eyebrow raised; Ben returned it with a look that said: *Don't say anything!* Justin was still getting used to the idea that vehicles, especially ambulances, could (sort of) hum a tune as well as talk.

"Denis? Is that you?"

"Yes, Ben, as always," Denis said with a small sigh. "Thanks for checking in. Where are you now?"

"Over Stonehenge."

"Right, there's an opportunity coming up for Justin to observe another crew. That ok with you?"

"Sure. Which one?"

"Give me a minute." Ben could hear Denis moving papers around the top of his desk. "Here we are. You're shadowing Bob and Michael. Set your co-ordinates for Exeter."

"Thanks, Denis. Over and out."

Justin looked out of the window, scanning the horizon. "How long will it take to get there?"

"Not long."

Justin suddenly exclaimed, "I know this part of the country!"

"Yes, the A303 is somewhere down there," replied Ben. "Not feeling a pang of regret are you?"

"Crikey, no. My accident is all past and almost forgotten. I'm much happier being here, with you and Clarissa."

"That's a good lad. Clarissa does like to be included in the conversation now and again."

They continued on course for Devon. Beneath them spread an undulating and beautiful landscape that today was basking in one of those special sunny summer's days that made you feel like a little bit of Heaven had managed to find its way to Earth.

Traffic was building up on the M5 motorway. "I think now's the time to keep an eye out," said Ben. "We're almost there. And remember, we're meant to be just observing. Get my drift?"

"Yes, ch... I mean, yes."

"Good." Ben smiled to himself. The lad was learning already.

"Here we go. Signal coming in. What is it Claris?"

"Motorway collision near Exeter. Bob knows you're on your way."

"Let him know we're nearly there and ready to provide back-up if necessary."

Ben looked across at Justin, whose face was flushed with excitement. "You shouldn't be getting excited about people dying you know," he admonished.

"Sorry," came the reply, "but this is my first time of doing anything like this."

"You mean being on the helping end?"

"Yes, I suppose that's what I mean. Never had a chance to help anyone before, especially not like this."

Ben banked the ambulance into a slow descent. Clarissa's location finder did the rest.

"Coming in to land," she said.

They didn't actually land on the ground, but instead hovered at Clarissa's usual parking spot some way above it, while they assessed the situation. It also meant they were out of the way of Bob's crew. Bob and

Michael knew Justin was new to all this, so they would do all they could not to throw him in at the deep end too quickly.

But all of a sudden, somebody yanked Justin's door open.

"'elp me, 'elp me," came the voice of somebody who was floating alongside of them. "Gawd Almighty, you're a bit high up!"

"Crikey," said Justin, looking a little alarmed. "Ben, what do I do?"

"Stay calm, that's the first thing. Grab the lady's hand and haul her in."

Justin did as he was told and the floating lady was soon sitting beside him in the cab.

"Thanks, dearie," she said, looking vastly relieved to be where she was, puffing out her plump, rosy cheeks and letting out a long sigh.

"Um," said Justin tentatively, "who are you? And what can we do for you?"

"I'm Chrissie, ducky," she laughed. "I saw yous coming an' I was never so 'cited in all me life. Well, in all me death I suppose you could say. Cor, what a laugh. I never thought I'd experience this. Well, y'know I've always believed people came to meet you, when you passes on that is, but this…. this is a real bonus. A real ride, in a real celestial ambulance."

"You've heard of us then?" said Ben, trying hard not to let his smile become an inane grin.

"Oh, yes, dearie. I was a clairvoyant, see. Me guides told me all about you lot…. and the *others*." She didn't enlighten them as to who the *others* were.

Justin was still in shock. This was so different from what he'd expected.

A signal came in from Bob. "We're ok down here. You can go home. Thanks."

"You're welcome, Bob. Any time. See you back at the depot."

Gently, Clarissa winged her way up into the blue yonder and beyond. The lady called Chrissie talked almost non-stop the whole way back, how she was so surprised they had come at just the right time. "I knew there was another accident, see, so I guessed they'd get priority. Nobody had cottoned on to what had happened to me, or so I thought. And then there you was. What a blessin', I said to meself. Thanks so much, ducky," she finished, patting Justin on the arm.

Justin for once was silenced and Ben was chuckling because of it. You never knew what was going to happen in this business.

Leaving Chrissie in the capable hands of the Sisters at the hospital, Ben caught sight of Harry, the airman. He was still helping out in whatever way he could.

"He's a lad for the ladies," Agnes commented. "But quite harmless, I'm glad to say, and he's actually quite helpful. So remember what I said about not encouraging him to become an ambulance man."

"As if I would," Ben grinned, wondering what Denis would say to someone like Harry joining the team.

"You know, Ben, I keep meaning to ask you how your education is coming along."

"Oh, just fine. I've met up with Horace a few times now and I had a recent excursion with Sam."

"Hmm," voiced Agnes, as if she knew Sam and his methods only too well. "No need to ask how that went."

"It was great. Sam's great! And he was so right. I learned lots about myself and things I thought I could never do. Sam said it was beginner's luck, but I thought I might have a certain knack for some things."

Agnes smiled. "Well you certainly have a knack for keeping an irascible ambulance happy. I've heard Clarissa has been quite full of herself lately, what with the excursion with Norman and his team and then going off with Sam."

"Yep, it's made me realise how much there is still to learn about how things work here."

"Have you enrolled at the university yet?"

"No. Denis found the missing forms, but then mislaid them again. I think they know I'm still undecided. The forms seem to have gone on voluntary walkabout."

Agnes grinned. "I canna believe Denis would lose them. He's so orderly. Well, after a fashion. I hope he finds them. They're enrolling soon."

Ben was surprised. He hadn't thought of timeframes being important, but maybe he was wrong.

Chrissie took to her new life like a duck to water. The Sisters loved her for her cheery smile and nature, and the other patients thought they had never met anyone quite like her.

And Justin? Well, after initially feeling a little shell-shocked meeting Chrissie, he recovered quickly, the general consensus at the station being that he had come through his first mission really well.

"Nothing like throwing them in at the deep end, eh, Ben?" Tom had commented back at the station. Ben thought Justin had handled everything better than expected. Chrissie was just a bit of a challenge for anyone on their first mission.

It wasn't so much later, on another of his frequent visits to check up on his 'patients', that Ben asked how Chrissie was faring.

"I think she's already discharged herself," said the ward orderly, Don. "Said there was nothing wrong with her that a good day's work couldn't cure. So she's gone off to the Market Place to get a job."

"Good for her! Wouldn't mind seeing what she ends up doing."

"Well, maybe she'll come back here to work. Ex-patients sometimes do."

Ben raised his eyebrows. "I didn't realise that."

"Oh yes. Once you've been here a bit longer you'll find out how many on the staff were once rescue cases. Well, Ben, it's nice chatting, but I've got a million and one things on my plate."

"And I need to get back to base," agreed Ben.

★

CHAPTER 14

A Special Life To Save

Ben headed for the ambulance station, still thinking about Chrissie and wondering where she would end up working. He scanned the station's notice board for any upcoming jobs - not an overlong list that scrolled down at a steady rate, deleting each mission as it was completed. Accidents, it seemed, were thankfully not so frequent just now. At the bottom there was one that hadn't yet been highlighted - highlighting meant a crew were out at the scene. A note in the margin said, 'To await an alert signal'. That meant a bell would sound for the next crew to go out, so it seemed this particular incident hadn't happened yet and might never happen; the circumstances surrounding the event were at that moment still in train. Incidents of any kind, not just accidents, could be avoided of course and then the list would change. Ben watched to see whether this particular one was ongoing or not.

Clarissa's engine was already warming up. She seemed to know when it was a good time to stay in readiness.

"You think we'll be called out to this one, if it happens?" asked Ben.

"Yes, I can feel it in my brake pads. They're ready to let go."

"Right, then I'd better buckle up. I know what you're like when you're ready to go. No stopping you, and you never check whether I'm ready or not."

Clarissa chuckled and then coughed and spluttered. Something was amiss, her timing was just a little out.

"Are you ok?" Ben asked, anxiously.

"Yes, but I think I'll get Frank to check under my bonnet when we get back. My last mission was a difficult one."

Ben had heard that she'd had to brave an etheric storm over London. Not an easy thing. It was all to do with too much electrical energy suddenly conflicting with natural atmospheric disruption, and Clarissa had been caught in the middle of it.

"It was a bit hairy," she confided. "Had to do a ninety degree turn to the right, then another to the left in quick succession. It was like trying to ride the crest of a gigantic wave in mid-ocean and in a howling storm."

"By the way, who was your driver?"

"Malcolm."

"Has he recovered yet?" Ben tried to suppress a grin.

"Oh yes, but he's sworn never to take me out again. He said some awful words afterwards. I had to muffle my air vents."

"Clarissa, are you sure it was just the electrical storm that caused you to swerve so drastically?"

"Oh, absolutely," she said in a very prim voice.

Suddenly the bell sounded loud and clear. Denis came running out of the station office. "Don't need an attendant for this one, Ben. Here are Clarissa's co-ordinates."

"Thanks," said Ben, logging them quickly onto Clarissa's navigational system. "No time to lose, girl."

He let out the brakes and Clarissa sailed off into the wide blue yonder, passing through the mist and into a heavy, gloomy sky. Thunder rolled in the distance. *Can't always expect it to be blue skies and sunshine,* he sighed.

"Heading north-by-north-west," intoned Clarissa, the navigational system showing they were making for a remote rural destination.

"Right Claris, take it steady, don't want another electrical glitch, do we?"

The storm was building up and although to all intents and purposes Clarissa and Ben were not visible to the human eye, the wind didn't know that, so it bumped and threw them around as if they were nothing more than a piece of damp tissue paper. Ben was glad his seat belt was firmly in place and that he'd never suffered from travel sickness.

Through misty curtains of rain he could see they were approaching a farmhouse. Clarissa's headlights were already on full beam as they landed softly on the driveway. It was safer than hovering in the air.

Seat belt unbuckled, Ben grabbed his first aid kit as he clambered out of the ambulance as fast as he could. "I might be back for more equipment Claris, so park as near to the door as possible, there's a good girl, and keep your headlights on. It looks as though the storm has cut the power."

It was true. The house was in total darkness except for two small gleams of light, one in an upstairs room, the other downstairs. Ben opened the front door, which was unlocked, although he could have drifted through without too much difficulty. Oak doors were not a special problem, though stone walls could be a bit tricky.

Low voices issued from the ground floor room to his left and someone, a woman he thought, was quietly crying. Ahead of him and standing at the bottom of the stairs, he was surprised to see a figure. A stranger to him, he nonetheless recognised an angel when he saw one. The angel had no wings, but a bright light emanated all around the figure in the shape of what you might call wings.

Blimey, this must be a special case.

The figure silently beckoned him to follow. Up the stairs they went and into a room lit by a solitary candle. The angel stood by the head of the bed and looked fondly down at its occupant, a very small boy. Standing over the boy with a stethoscope in his ears was the local doctor. He wore a worried frown on his face, pursing his lips as he felt for the feeble pulse of life issuing from the boy's heart.

The angel signalled to Ben to come across to the other side of the bed. Once there, Ben immediately opened up the first aid kit, reaching instinctively for a small phial in one of the pockets. The angel shook his head and indicated that another phial would be better. Filling a small syringe with the translucent liquid, Ben gently inserted the needle into a vein in the boy's left arm.

Very shortly, the expression on the doctor's face began to change to one of hopefulness, as the little boy's chest began to rise and fall with deeper breaths. The guardian angel radiated a pearly white ray that spread over the whole of the small body on the bed. Atoms and molecules bubbled and fizzed like soda pop.

The angel signalled again that there was one more thing to do. Following instructions, Ben pulled out a large wad of lint, pouring over it the contents of the first phial he had chosen. Then, placing it very gently on the little boy's chest, he secured it with invisible tape. There would be no need to remove the pad, because once it had done its job it would, like the tape, gradually dissolve back into the ether from whence it had come. The angel looked pleased, and Ben felt a lovely warm feeling wash over him as the words "Well done" echoed in his head.

"You're very welcome," he replied, "and thank you for *your* help, too."

"The boy is a special case," said the angel. "He could have passed on at this age, but pulling him through his illness will be of more benefit, not just for him but for others as well. It has come to our attention lately that he has volunteered to do an important job on Earth, so we wanted to make sure he stayed."

Ben smiled, and wondered what this boy would do with his life that was so special. For the briefest moment that seemed strangely long enough, Ben was given the privilege of seeing what could happen in this small boy's future life. He saw him on the world stage, though not in a political role. His task would be to bring nations together without ever having to be part of a governing body.

"He will be an inspiration to those he meets. He will be an ideas person, who can see beyond problems and present solutions. He will have a strong ethic and gentle heart, one of the new generation that will lead people towards peace. He cannot, of course, do this on his own. There'll be others like him who he will work with."

Ben hoped with all his heart that the boy would live and accomplish all that his life promised him.

The doctor was now smiling broadly and looking vastly relieved that he hadn't lost a patient. Doctors always seemed to blame themselves if that happened, when really they didn't have the last word at all.

"Right, then," Ben said to the angel, "I guess my task is done here. I'll be off if it's ok with you."

The angel smiled and bade him farewell. "I shall stay a little longer."

When Ben left the house, he saw Clarissa had turned around and had her engine running smoothly, ready for take-off.

"Well, Claris, that's another good ending. How about we head home? I need a cup of tea."

"We could get one on the way."

"Oh? Where?"

"Well there's a certain ambulance station that we both know and they're just changing shifts, so you know what that means!"

"Yes, the kettle will be on. Tell me, Claris, where we're going, is there a chance I might see someone I know?"

"Uh-huh. And I might meet a few friends, too."

"What, the other ambulances? They won't be able to see you, will they?"

"Oh, you'd be surprised what they can see. They'll know me for sure. And I can pass on some gossip from the other stations I've visited."

"What other stations? Claris, what have you been up to in your spare time?"

"Oh, just tuning my frequencies into theirs."

"Is that allowed?"

"Well, it isn't *not* allowed, if you see what I mean."

"That's because nobody knows you're doing it. I bet the other ambulances don't know it either."

"Oh, them! They don't know their front end from their boot, them!"

Ben chuckled quietly to himself. It wouldn't do to make Clarissa think he approved of her little whims.

They soared up into the sky, the storm abating. A pale crescent moon hid intermittently behind scudding clouds that seemed in a hurry to keep up with the storm. Hung like a half-made paper lantern in the velvety blackness of a rural sky, the moon shone a welcome light, heralding a calmer night, and pin cushion stars pricked out their eternal designs.

Finally, destination in sight, Clarissa began their slow descent. She was looking forward to meeting her friends, as was Ben, even though they wouldn't have a clue he was there. And the cup of tea? Well, he could make his own.

★

CHAPTER 15

Chrissie And The Children

"Plenty of crews in at the moment," said the station's super. "We know where to find you if we need you."

"Is Brian around, Denis?" Ben hadn't seen his friend around for a while and wanted to catch up with him. Brian had been with him on his very first mission, helping him to settle into a role that secretly everyone knew he would fit into very easily, once his confidence was restored.

"No, mate, hasn't been around here for a little while."

"Yes, I've noticed."

"You'll catch him at the hospital, though, for sure. He seems to have taken up temporary residence there."

A nurse directed Ben to Ward IVB. "Hardly ever leaves the place," she said, grinning.

"So that's why I haven't seen him at the station. Doesn't he work for us any more?"

"His epaulettes changed colour. Didn't you notice?"

Ben thought about it and realised he hadn't. But then they had often been on missions at different times and missed seeing each other.

"Over here," a familiar voice called out. "This is Ben," Brian said to a patient. "He's on one of the crews who help people like yourself. Ben, this is Mavis. She's only been in a little while, but she's coming on in leaps and bounds."

The woman smiled, a patient smile that whispered *I'm not quite better yet, but I know I'm in the right place.* "I'm pleased to meet you," she murmured finally, her voice still a bit croaky, her body still frail, needing time.

"Pleased to meet you too, Mavis. You're in good hands here, luv."

"Oh, I know," she replied, casting a fond glance in Brian's direction.

"Falling in love with this rogue are you?" joked Ben.

"Well, he's the best hunk I've seen since I arrived. Oh!" she added shyly, "I shouldn't have said that."

"Why not?" said Brian. "It's the best offer I've had for ages!"

Mavis laughed. And what began as a thin cackle quickly turned into something more vibrant, more alive. "You'll do," Brian said to her softly. "Now you just rest. I'll check in on you later."

No sooner were these words uttered than she closed her eyes and fell asleep, a soft white ray wrapping around her limp body, a featherlight coverlet encircling her in a balm of healing. Brian and Ben walked quietly away.

"Fancy a coffee?" asked Ben.

"No thanks. Gave that up a while ago, but I'll come along for a chat."

"That's not all you've given up. Where's your uniform?"

"Not needed, like the coffee."

"I can understand you might want to give up coffee, but heavens, Brian, you've given up the ambulance service too?"

"I've moved on, which is why I was pleased to see you. I wanted to let you know what I was doing."

"A nurse told me your epaulettes had changed colour. So what does that mean, and how... why do epaulettes change colour? Are they meant to? I mean, do you know when, or *what*?" Ben looked at his own as if he thought they might drop off his jacket at any minute. They were, however, still very determinedly silver and still very determinedly attached to his uniform.

"It only happens when you're ready. It's a sort of promotion, but not a promotion, if you know what I mean. It's the next step." Brian gave his friend a moment to digest this new information. "Don't be in a hurry, mate. They will only change if you're needed elsewhere. And then it's your decision where you will end up."

Ben cocked an eyebrow disbelievingly. "So far I haven't noticed that anyone had a say in their own preferences. Least of all me!"

Brian laughed. "Well, I've never been able to fault the reasoning of those who know better than us. Anyway, I'm not just helping out at the hospital, I'm also enrolled at the university, doing something about my education."

"Education! God, Brian, that's what I'm meant to be doing. Only I'm a bit nervous about it."

"Well, you'll find it is so totally different from any schooling you had on Earth you couldn't possibly not enjoy it. I love it, and if you'd asked me before I went I would have said wild horses couldn't have dragged me there. But there, you see, those that help us make up our minds know better. Given the chance you should take it. It will broaden your knowledge of... well, everything."

"You sound like a convert, Brian, and I trust what you say. But what if I don't fit in, can't do the lessons? I always considered myself a hands-on man, not a student."

"All the first-timers will be the same, like you. Nearly everyone seems to choose something that's a challenge for them, not necessarily something they will find the easiest option."

"Oh, the *challenge*!" quipped Ben. "It will certainly be that for me." Ben fingered a loose button, thinking he must see Steve to get it fixed.

Brian eyed him for a minute then placed a hand on Ben's shoulder. "How about that coffee?"

They translocated in the blink of an eye and both sat for a while in companionable silence, Brian lost in a reverie of his own while Ben waited for his hot drink to cool. He'd changed his mind and ordered ginger and lemon. Maybe it would help him give up coffee.

"So what's it like working at the hospital?"

"Well, no need for me to tell you how great it is. The best bit, though, is that I'm beginning to understand more about the hospital's role. Even though it's officially called the Lodge of Rest and Recuperation, souls passing over don't just come for a rest. Sometimes they need something more. I had a case recently where this guy came in completely devoid of any emotion. He had it all so bottled up thinking it wasn't manly to show feelings. Sister Ecstatica sorted it out though. Gave him a good talking to, in that way she has of being angelic but to the point."

"Oh yes, I've come across Sister Ecstatica. She's a real gem, but she doesn't take long to tell you exactly what you need to hear."

"In the nicest possible way, of course."

Ben grinned. "I guess she's the one they can count on to deal with awkward cases."

"She has a knack of mending their souls as well as their spirit. Anyway, what do you think you will do when it's time for you to move on?"

"You mean if my epaulettes change colour? I don't know, to be truthful. I've just assumed I would always be at the ambulance station. Anyway, I couldn't leave Clarissa, could I?"

"I've heard she's taken quite a shine to you, lucky man. She used to be a real tearaway sometimes."

"Still is, but she grows on you. Brian, this education stuff, you think I'd be ok at it? I've heard they expect you to make the commitment, take it seriously."

"Yes, well, as far as that goes. They have to remind you that you're not there to waste anybody's time. Once you've set your mind to something it's expected you'll be able to finish what you have started."

"I'm still not sure about it all. Never was much good at the academic side of things, but it feels like I can't keep putting off the inevitable."

Brian smiled knowingly. "I'm glad you're thinking about it at least. Any idea of a choice of subject?"

"I thought anything medical would be great, a step up perhaps from what an ambulance man needs to know. But there are a few hoops to go through first."

"You need to meet up with Doug. He's good on the medical front."

Ben sipped his ginger and lemon thoughtfully; it was spicy and tart with a hidden sweetness. He wondered how they did that, whoever *they* were. Or was it just his thought form that had created it the way he liked it? He shook his head at his imaginings. There were other more important things to think about than how his drink had been made.

"I believe there's an Orientation Day at the Halls of Learning and I can attend that once I've filled in the enrolment forms. There's a chance I could get in for the next intake."

Brian clapped Ben on the shoulder. "That's really great. Hmm, let me see... next semester, that will be in two parsecs."

"You've been watching *Star Trek* movies, too, then!"

"Used to love them. You know, we have a place over here where they provide all the ideas for the writers down on Earth."

"Doesn't surprise me. Though, no, I didn't know."

"It's in the Arts Department of the Halls of Learning, known as the *Rooms of Volumes*."

"Do they ever run out of space? Must be an awful lot of information stored there."

"Yes, well, don't ask me. Don't know much about the technical stuff of all that, but it's a fascinating place. You can even watch movies of stories that will eventually turn up at the end of someone's pen, or in front of someone's movie camera."

"Now that's what I call hot off the press!"

They laughed. "Right, Ben, as you are on your free time and I can't hear Sister Ecstatica calling me back to the hospital, I think we have a little time to take a trip. It seems the perfect moment."

And in the twinkling of an eye they were both in a place Ben had never visited before.

"Where are we?"

"It's called The Children's Area."

"And what are we doing here?"

"Trust me, you'll love it," reassured Brian. "And anyway there's someone here who's keen to see you again." Ben looked blankly at his friend; he couldn't think of anyone he knew who worked with children.

Even though he had never had children of his own, he thought he would like them, especially after the visit with Sam to Matron Agatha's orphanage. His only worry was whether these children would be even more exuberant than the orphans. And would they be too much to handle? He liked a quiet, laid back life, though thinking about it his present existence wasn't the slippers-and-pipe fantasy he had once pictured for himself. That fiction vanished a long time ago.

"Here we are," announced Brian. In front of them was what looked like a small hamlet of cottages amidst green, undulating farm land. And then, like corks popping out of several bottles, out of a barn ran an excited gang of free-range children, all heading in their direction.

"Hold your horses, you youngsters," cried Brian as they threw themselves at him, vying for any sort of hug it was possible to get with so many of them and only one of him.

"Now, come on," he said, "give me time to introduce you to my friend. This is Ben. Ben, these are the children of the Summerland."

They all stared at Ben and then grinned, throwing themselves off Brian and onto Ben's stalwart figure, nearly knocking him over.

"They're an animated bunch, aren't they?" Ben quipped.

"That's a good word – animated! I'll have to mention that to the ladies who look after them. I'm sure they'd agree."

A stately lady of good height, hair neatly tied into a bun on the nape of her neck was walking towards them. The two men uncoiled themselves from the children, Ben following Brian's lead as they both stood very straight and to attention.

"This is Miranda," said Brian, and then out of the corner of his mouth added, "She used to be a teacher on Earth. Quite traditional, she nonetheless has a heart of marshmallow."

"Hello, Miranda."

"Hello, Brian. And who do I have the pleasure of being introduced to?"

"This is Ben, Miranda. Ben works at the ambulance station."

"Good Lord. Do you like it? I shouldn't like attending accidents myself. You brave man."

Ben smiled and shook her hand. "Well, I'm used to it. It's what I did when I was on Earth."

"Oh," Miranda said, nodding her head as if that explained it all. "Come, come, let me show you around. This is your first time here I take it? I haven't seen you before."

"Yes, first time. It looks ... "

"Familiar and charming? Too charming for hectic children?"

"Well, yes. Not what I expected really. A hamlet? Farmyards?"

"Well, we change it from time to time, but at the moment the children are learning about how to keep animals, so obviously a farm is a good idea. Mind you, they're also learning about wild things and how to work in harmony with nature. We teach them to revere all life, no matter what its size or shape. All life is productive and mutually supportive. The hope is that when they return to Earth they will have a heightened appreciation of all living things."

Ben nodded, appreciative of this insight into the way knowledge was imparted to the children. He began to wonder about his own future education.

And then a familiar face appeared.

"Chrissie!" Ben exclaimed. "Well I never!"

"Hello, ducks. Didn't expect me to end up `ere, did you?"

"Well, no, but then I hadn't particularly pictured you anywhere."

Chrissie laughed, a deep throaty sound that came from somewhere deep in her stomach and rose up to her throat, growing in intensity as it went, shaking her whole body.

"Oh dear," she said finally, wiping a tear from her eye, "that's a good'un and no mistake. `adn't pictured me anywhere! Well, I can tell you this is perfick for me. Luv it. Kids, animals, sweet li'l cottages, farmyards without the smell... Absolutely perfick."

Miranda was smiling. Straight-backed as always, unbending, yet her smile was full of warmth and tenderness. Ben could see she appreciated Chrissie and her sense of humour.

"Chrissie, would you like to show Ben and Brian around? It's Ben's first time."

"Gawd luv yer. `Course I will. Can't leave them standing `ere like dumb clucks, now can we? Come on lads, let's do the tour."

Ben grinned inanely and Brian had to turn his head sideways trying to suppress an urge to laugh out loud. In the end it was no contest otherwise he would have burst a blood vessel. They all began to laugh then, the children too.

Eventually recovering themselves, Brian, Ben and Chrissie marched off on the tour. Ben could see that Chrissie loved showing people around as much as she loved the children.

"Did you have children, Chrissie?" asked Ben.

"Gawd, yes, only they weren't me own. Looked after waifs and strays mostly. Some parents aren't always able to look after their own prop'ly. Now, where was we? Oh, yes, the workshop."

They entered one of the barns situated on the edge of the hamlet. Outside, cows mooed, pigs snuffled and chickens clucked. It had all the appearance of a conventional Earthly rural landscape.

Inside the barn was much activity with more children all busy at their various tasks. A teacher, who they were introduced to as Carmella, was encouraging the children to use their creativity. The youngsters worked with whatever materials were at hand; some familiar to Ben like pieces of wood, pens, pencils, paper, straw, sand, and metals of all shapes and sizes, and others that ... well, weren't, and he had no way of naming them. Computers were allowed, it appeared, and each child had access to their own console, inputting information and ideas from the hands-on play. They were being inventive, broadening their minds to limitless possibilities. It was science and art without the laboratories or classrooms.

Chrissie then took the *lads* as she called him and Brian, out to one of the cottages. There the children's creativity was being given full expression as they practised visualising their perfect home. Instead of using paints on canvas or paper, they concentrated on an idealised picture in their mind, allowing their thoughts to influence the etheric particles of the world they lived in. Imagination brought form into reality. Ben and Brian were amused at the way the children experimented with various colours and textures, changing at a whim floor coverings, furniture, colours of walls. It was improvisation taken to a level that could never be achieved on Earth, and it was also great fun.

"It 'elps 'em to reco'nise their own personality and character, as well as fine-tuning any talent they may 'ave." And then Chrissie's voice changed a little, as she continued on, saying: "Surprising how creativity can help to know yourself at a deeper level. We don't encourage the children to conform to someone else's idea of what's right or wrong. Instead, they're encouraged to see their own ideas as bringing in a multiplicity of energy."

Ben and Brian looked aghast as Chrissie uttered these words of wisdom.

"Or somefink like that," she added in her old voice. "Y'know, what benefits not only them but everyfink 'round 'em."

"My, Chrissie, you know how to spout the wisdom!" commented Brian.

"And you said it beautifully," added Ben.

Chrissie brightened. "Well it's slow, but I'm beginning to refine myself just a little round the edges. Oh!" she said, as if in answer to an unasked question, "I won't change me personality, but it's nice to be able to show people that you know what you're talking about, instead of fudging it."

Ben noticed that Chrissie's voice had changed, becoming softer and deeper. He realised then that she had greeted them initially as her old self, so they would feel more comfortable and wouldn't be too surprised at the change in her. Besides which, *she* was still coming to terms with this newly developing side of herself.

"Fancy a cup of tea?" she asked.

"Oh, yes," said both of the men.

"I thought you'd given it up?" queried Ben.

"Not tea!" said Brian. "Never give up a cup of tea."

And so Chrissie, Ben and Brian sat on a bale of straw and watched as birds and butterflies swooped and fluttered in the bright sunshine – a light that never hurt the eyes, only warmed the soul to its deepest contentment.

"Gawd, what a luverly place," said Chrissie, slipping back into her old self.

Ben guffawed into his tea, nearly spilling it all over himself, and Brian went off for a walk through the woods to save his facial muscles from cramping up altogether.

"That woman will be the death of me!" he was heard to exclaim.

"Is he all right do you think?" asked Chrissie.

Ben answered eventually. "Yes, luv. I just don't think he has ever come across anyone like you before."

"Gawd 'elp those that follow then. By the way," Chrissie continued, her voice changing again, "how's Justin? Lovely lad."

"He's getting on famously. Puts in for extra shifts all the time. Can't get enough of this rescue work."

"How did he die? I mean how did he get here?"

"Fell off a motorbike."

"Go on," she said, "must've been worse than that."

"Yeah, it was an accident on the A303."

"Busy road. And the way it narrows, just as you've got used to the dual carriageway. Wonder if they'll ever do anything about that?" It was a rhetorical question.

"Chrissie, I never found out how you came to be passing by our ambulance. You'd obviously given up the ghost, but how?"

"Got in the path of an oncoming tractor, dearie – just off the A303 - and I came off second best. I'm a Londoner, so country driving was a bit new, 'specially down those narrow lanes with lots of blind corners. Lucky yous was in the area."

"Yes, though we were there for quite a different reason. But you did give Justin a shock," said Ben, smiling at the memory.

"What d'you think he'll end up doing? Can't see him staying in the ambulance service, if you don't mind me saying."

"I think you might be right, Chrissie. He's got a lot going for him. Still very young in lots of ways, but eager. I expect he'll be getting some education sooner rather than later."

"I've heard about this education. Came as a bit of a shock."

"To me, too."

"I haven't been contacted yet. But I'm happy to stay here with the children. Learning lots from them. Children are amazing teachers, you know. Just watching them helps to understand how the human mind works. Gawd, it's completely irrational!"

They both giggled.

Suddenly Ben could sense a signal in his mind. He was improving with his telepathic skills and this had the true ring of a message from the ambulance station.

"Got to go," he said. "Would love to see you again, Chrissie. Mind if I bring Justin along too?"

"Bring whoever you like, dearie. We love getting visitors."

Ben gave Chrissie a big hug. "I'll try and persuade Justin."

Chrissie giggled. "Does he like wild children?"

"Sure to. He's been one himself, I bet."

It was time to leave. One more glance at Chrissie as a fond farewell, and before he and Brian knew it they were both back at the ambulance station. Ben made straight for the office as Brian waved farewell and disappeared into the ether.

★

CHAPTER 16

The Missing Girl

Behind Denis's rather large desk sat Steve, sewing a silver button on a jacket. The desk was strewn with other items of uniform needing repair, as well as an assortment of engine parts.

"Hi Steve. Didn't expect to see you here."

"I'm filling in."

"Denis might be a bit upset when he sees all this stuff on his desk."

"Oh, won't take a moment to clear this lot up."

"He's not back yet, then? Not out looking for more recruits?"

Steve snorted. "No, none of that. Said he was taking time off to visit a friend who's a nurse at the hospital."

"Didn't know he knew any of the nurses. He's very spare with personal information."

Steve grinned. "Always been like that, ever since I've known him."

"You go back a long while then?"

"Knew him before we came here. He was my Dad."

"Well, I'll be blowed!" said Ben, somewhat taken aback. "You know, I'd never have guessed you were father and son. And now you've both ended up working together."

"Well, we don't exactly work side by side but, yes, we chose to be here together. Dad of course came first and was waiting for me when I arrived. It was a wonderful reunion because on Earth we had never really seen eye-to-eye, but suddenly every hurt or disappointment melted away as soon as we saw each other. He's a great person and as long as we don't bump into each other too often, we seem to get on." Steve's laughter lines twitched slightly. "We finally found companionship after a life fraught with incompatibility."

"Do you hang out together?"

"Sometimes, but we like to do different things with our leisure time. I like to do a spot of gardening, while Dad prefers visiting the local dog kennels – he loves helping the people who look after them. The dogs there are all recovering from a previous life where they weren't treated very well... you know what can sometimes happen. And of course we both make time to keep an eye on Mum. You see, I came over early on and she's still over there."

There was a pause and Steve continued sewing on silver buttons. Ben knew that feeling, remembering those who were still on Earth.

"Once a tailor, always a tailor," Steve said finally, breaking the moment.

"And the engine parts?"

"Oh, those. I'm a bit faddy about keeping things in good condition. Dave brings them in when they get overloaded with other jobs. He knows I like cleaning them."

Ben wondered why anyone in the Summerland would need to be bothered with cleaning. Didn't stuff just clean itself? He never needed to have a bath, or use a bathroom now he came to think of it. Perhaps some old habits just hung on?

He looked at Steve as he sat contented with his sewing and realised there was still a lot he didn't understand about this new life of his. Steve looked younger than Denis. No, that was wrong, Steve certainly looked young, but then Denis didn't look old, just perhaps more mature. Maturity always showed through somehow, especially in the early days of being here. After that it seemed everyone chose their favourite age, and stuck to it, or that's what he'd heard. As for himself, he still thought he was fifty-something. There were no mirrors to tell him different, though to tell the truth he *felt* thirty-something.

"You're good at fixing engines, too, I've heard."

"Hmm, you're not wrong, though I thought I'd be driving the ambulances, not patching them up."

Ben chuckled because he knew darned well Steve loved what he was doing and if anyone had tried to prise him away from his job they would have known all about it.

"Anything for me that you know of?"

Steve looked up from his needle and thread. "Um, let's see." He shifted a few engine parts out of the way and plucked at a piece of paper that was at that moment in danger of disappearing under more engine parts that had appeared randomly out of thin air. "Too many," he voiced rather loudly, as if someone the other side of the station would hear. "That Harold, forgets I'm already inundated with work. Here you are. Clarissa's fuelled up and ready to go and you've got Justin going along with you as attendant. Ok?"

"Yes, mate. Thanks."

Justin was already in the passenger seat, chatting away to Clarissa, who was clearly beginning to have quite an attachment to the young lad if not absolutely adoring him; well, that is, not more than Ben, but perhaps almost as much. Justin looked as fresh-faced as ever, with plenty of mischief written all over his face. On his knees was a wad of papers.

"What've you been talking to Claris about?" asked Ben.

"My stories."

"Stories? What stories?"

Justin pointed to the papers on his lap. "Oh, just some scribblings. Don't mean much right now."

"What are you writing about, if you don't mind me asking?"

"My experiences."

"What? You mean you've found enough to write about even in the short time you've been here? Blimey, you're a fast track'un and no mistake. So what are these stories about?"

"People I've met."

Ben looked sideways at Justin and wondered what sort of a character he'd been cast as. "I suppose that includes me?" he quipped.

"Yes. Do you mind?"

Ben laughed. "No, not in the least, as long as I get first chance to have a look at what you've written. Might need some editing."

"Oh no, I've said some good things about you. No need."

"Well, Justin, just the same I'd like to have a look. How far have you got with it?"

Justin picked up the sheaf of papers and flicked over the pages as if he was quickly calculating how many there were. "I've done about five case studies."

"Oh, it's case studies is it?" Ben was still smiling, shaking his head gently from side to side as he buckled up. "Time to get going, I think. And while we're travelling you can tell me who else you've chosen to be a case study - and what you're going to do with your writing when you've finished."

"I'm looking for a publisher," replied Justin in a serious voice.

"Well, you won't get many up here who can help you, unless you just want the stories to go straight to the *Rooms of Volumes*."

"I've been talking to someone who works there," said Justin. Ben was surprised. Not everyone was that presumptuous. The *Rooms of Volumes* were like holy ground to most souls. They were the repositories for everything that ever happened, had form, had memory.

"Yes," Justin carried on. "His name's Sam and he said he'd be interested in my work and that I should show him when I've completed the first book."

"Book? Wow, Justin, you've really got the bit between your teeth. A book is a substantial amount of writing. Didn't think you had it in you."

"Sam says there's a special office that deals with publishing. The Future Stories Office, or something."

"A department of the *Rooms of Volumes*, no doubt."

"Sam says sometimes people on Earth pick up on what is written up here."

"Ghost-writing then?" grinned Ben.

"Yes," laughed Justin, "you could say that."

"Good lad. Keep it up. And buckle up your seat belt, please, while we're at it. We're about to take off."

Justin looked pleased with the encouragement, buckling up as quickly as he could.

"And, by the way," said Ben, "Sam's a good man, if he's the one I'm thinking of."

"He said he knew you." Ben smiled broadly.

Clarissa took off as usual, straight up into the air at an acute angle of seventy degrees. Ben's mind was still thinking about the editors at the *Rooms of Volumes* and what they might think of Justin's case studies, when all of a sudden Clarissa's klaxon sounded loud and clear.

"Emergency ahead," she announced.

Ben shook himself as if waking from a dream. Where was he and why wasn't he paying attention? He soon came to his senses, though, checking the screen on the dashboard for information. Justin had put his writing away neatly into the glove compartment and was getting ready to unbuckle his seat belt.

"Hang on, Justin, let's get down nearer the ground first. Ok Claris, let's do it."

"Sandy beach below," Clarissa pointed out. "Small group of people standing around a body. Not sure of condition of patient."

The beach came into view, and sure enough there was a small group of people huddled together, heads bent over someone. Ben could see two feet protruding slightly from the group.

"Ok, Justin, this one's all yours. Think you can handle it?"

"Sure thing," came the confident reply.

Cockiness aside, Justin was shaping up to be a first-class ambulance attendant. He always kept his uniform neat and combed his hair before coming on duty. As he had difficult, floppy hair and a lot of it, this was to his credit. Ben smiled inwardly and sat back for a moment watching his attendant get to work. It wasn't easy as the group of onlookers were in the way, leaving little space for Justin to manoeuvre himself close enough to the person needing his attention. As a last resort he tunnelled between the legs of one particularly tall onlooker.

In front of him, completely comatose if not actually dead, was a very lovely-looking young woman, probably in her twenties, he thought. Her clothes were very wet. One of the group was kneeling beside her, trying all the resuscitation techniques he could remember. It was a long time since he'd done any first aid training and what he knew wasn't working. He was sweating and exhausted.

Justin rapidly got to work, doing what he could to save the woman. Out of his first aid kit he took a small gadget that worked like a pump, except it looked nothing like you would expect a pump to look like: a box-like contraption that glowed incandescently as if a light were burning inside. He rummaged in the first aid kit again and pulled out a thin silvery tube, attached it to the pump and inserted the other end into the young woman's mouth.

Minutes ticked by. There was no response. Justin then reached into his kit for a small phial, opening the box-like pump and adding another invisible ingredient to the gaseous mixture. But it made no difference. He looked back through the tall man's legs at Ben, who was still sitting in the ambulance. With a nod of his head, Ben understood what Justin was feeling.

"I won't be long, Claris. Keep an eye on the tide. I think it's turning."

As Ben walked down the beach to where Justin was now sitting just outside the circle of onlookers, he wondered whether the people were still there through some inherent human compassion; they couldn't leave her, even though she was well past anyone's help. Did they wish, even, that their combined presence might somehow change the reality of the situation? Or perhaps they lingered, not knowing what else to do?

Justin looked forlorn and dejected. "You can't save them all," Ben said, laying a hand reassuringly on the young man's shoulder. "She's gone. Let her physical body be. Our prime concern now is to go looking for her spirit. She's wandered off whilst nobody was looking and most likely she'll be needing our help."

Justin wiped away a tear that had slid unbidden down his cheek. "Right, guv. Yes, she'll be needing our assistance in a different way, won't she?" He'd taken her loss personally. He'd learn.

Justin packed up his first aid kit and without wasting any more time he and Ben left the little group of onlookers behind them. Already the sound of an Earthly ambulance was getting nearer and nearer.

Justin jumped into the attendant's seat and closed the door in a quick, fluid movement that lost no time and reflected his mood perfectly. Ben knew what was coming next.

"Where shall we start first? I want to find her and I won't rest until I do."

"What do you suggest?" queried Ben.

"Perhaps Clarissa could help?"

"Well, why don't you ask her?"

Justin pressed the communicator button on the dashboard and cleared his throat. "Clarissa, I've got... We've got an important request."

"Yes, Justin, what is it?"

"We've lost one of our patients."

A muffled giggle.

"It's not funny, Claris," said Ben.

"Sorry."

"We think you could help. She's out there somewhere. We just need to be the first ones to find her. Justin here wants to get a gold star, added to which he seems to have formed quite an attachment to her."

"No, I haven't, guv," stammered Justin, going bright red. "I just don't like to think of her getting lost, that's all. Feel a bit responsible, that's all."

"Ok, Justin, didn't mean to upset you. Right, Claris, it's up to you. Let's up and away and have a good look from above. She can't have gone far."

Up soared Clarissa into the quickly darkening sky. Rain clouds were forming overhead. She switched on her headlights to full beam and the sky lit up with brilliant clarity. Ben manoeuvred her carefully so that they floated just beneath the clouds. Away from the beach, the traffic beneath was moving at a steady pace, on roads that crisscrossed the countryside like childish scrawls on scrap paper.

"Picking up a signal," said Clarissa suddenly.

Ben and Justin looked not only straight ahead, but also out of the side windows. It wasn't the ground they were looking at, but the sky between what was below and what was above; and before long, there in the headlights, they found her, a wisp of her former self, floating aimlessly in the ether. Clarissa quickly changed down to a lower gear, as Justin was already jumping out of the passenger door and heading towards the young woman.

She turned in fright at the bright light in her eyes and the shapes that were coming towards her.

"Go away!" she cried in panic.

"It's all right, we're here to help," said Justin in a comforting voice.

"That's what the others said, except they only wanted to make fun of me!"

"We won't do that, luv," Justin added in his most appealing voice. "We're the good guys, anyway."

"Good guys, bad guys, I don't know what you're doing here anyway. All I want to do is go home. And I'm soaking wet too… through and through."

Justin had brought a blanket with him, which he carefully and gently put around her shoulders, at the same time guiding her back towards Clarissa, who by now had found a convenient place to park. Ben was already starting to brew a cup of tea. He desperately needed one, too, as the atmosphere had become decidedly chilly - no doubt due to the *others* the young woman had inadvertently met. He knew who they were – waifs of the underworld.

"You're not real paramedics are you?" she queried.

"Well, we are and we aren't," said Justin.

"I think what Justin means," said Ben, "is that we also help people, but not in exactly the same way."

The young woman looked at the two men, one not exactly older, but looking more experienced than the other. She noticed their uniforms were a bit out of the ordinary, wrong colour as well as style for a start, but then she was having difficulty remembering what she thought a paramedic *should* wear. And, come to think of it, why wasn't she hooked up to some life-saving equipment?

Before she could think another thought, Ben, using his gentlest voice said, "We can't bring you back to the life you once knew, but we can assure you that where we're going is a lot better."

"Yes," she said, "I know. I know what you mean. I've died haven't I?"

Justin squeezed her hand and she looked up then and smiled into his eyes.

"Oh dear," groaned Ben to himself, "that's done it!" He felt, however, it would be wise for the moment to keep the conversation going, even though he was with two people who seemed to have lost consciousness of anything except each other.

"You've passed over. It always comes as a surprise if you're not expecting it, but you'll soon get the hang of everything, and you'll love it."

The young woman managed to detach her gaze from Justin, and also her hand, as Ben passed her a cup of tea. "Thank you," she said. Then an awful thought crossed her mind. "But what about…?"

Ben knew immediately what her concern was. "Don't worry about your folks. We'll talk some more about how you can help them. Now, there's nothing to be done except to get you out of here and back home."

Warming her hands on her cup, the young woman began to relax. "It's really easy isn't it?" she said finally. "I mean, it's just like falling off a log."

Ben smiled to himself. Well, that was one way of putting it.

Justin fussed around, making sure she was comfortable and warm. Her clothes were drying out quickly now.

At the Lodge of Reception and Recuperation it was Justin who handed their patient over to the Sisters. Sister Ruth was on duty and she had quite a time disengaging him from the young woman, who he had by now found out was called Carol.

"She'll be fine now, *thank you*, Justin," said the Sister, as she prised his hand away from Carol's arm.

"Are you sure?" Justin asked. "She's had a nasty shock you know. Still a bit wobbly."

"Yes, Justin, I do know how people feel when they first arrive." Sister Ruth then relented a little, allowing Justin to take Carol into the ward; but once there the nurse was all business and discipline, and gave Justin his final marching orders. "You're needed elsewhere young man, and don't you forget it."

"Yes, Sister," he replied, swivelling his head around to make sure Carol *was* really ok.

Ben thought the two of them would be seeing a lot more of each other in future, that's if Justin didn't smother her with affection first. *I'll have to have a word. He'll put her off if he's not careful. She needs time to adjust.*

Justin hopped back into the ambulance and started whistling under his breath.

"Everything ok then?" remarked Ben.

"Couldn't be better," replied Justin.

"Now lad, there's just a little bit of advice I need to give you..."

Clarissa hummed a little tune. Ben and Justin had gone for a cup of tea and a man-to-man talk. She smiled to herself in a motorised sort of way. It had been another fulfilling day and she felt nicely tired, not exhausted, not overheated, just relishing the comfort of relaxing her brake pads and shifting into neutral gear. Her springs sagged a little and she let out a contented sigh. She was happy and she thought Ben was too. But at the back of her mind was the fact that there would come a time in the future when Ben's epaulettes would change colour and she suddenly felt sad. What would become of her then? Would Ben decide to stay on and continue to work with the rescue service? Or would he take the chance to move on to other things? Her engine coughed two or three times. It was the nearest thing to crying that she could manage.

"I must be brave," she thought. "There will be other drivers and attendants." But she knew there would never be another Ben. She lifted her headlights to see Ben walking over towards her. Straight away he knew something was not quite right.

"Eh-up, madam, what's wrong? You look all sort of... sad."

"Oh, it's nothing, Ben. Really."

"Now, come on old girl, it has to be something. I've never seen your bumper so low to the ground before. Tell me. What is it?"

"Well," she began, and then coughed though only in a small way, as she didn't want Ben to know how sad she really was. "I was just wondering how long it would be before your epaulettes started to change colour. That would mean you'd have the chance to move on and do other things... and... and I think I'm going to miss you." Her engine coughed again a couple of times.

"Oh, Claris, don't you fret. I'm not going anywhere just yet, even if my epaulettes did change colour. Anyway what could I possibly do that wouldn't include you?" Ben placed his hand on her bonnet and stroked her paintwork gently; but inwardly he had to confess he was excited at the prospect of what might happen one day. And then he began to think about all the people he and Clarissa had helped and he knew that he couldn't give up that sort of work so easily. It was such a gift, being able to help people in that way, and he'd made some good friends at the station, friends he'd always want to keep in touch with.

He stroked Clarissa's bonnet again and said, "Don't you worry, old girl. You and me, we're made for each other."

Clarissa's headlights swivelled to the side, trying to catch sight of Ben and let him know how grateful she was for his kind words. "We shall see, Ben. After all it's not up to you or me. Is it?"

"Well, let's not think about it just for now. There's more to be done, and if you're ready I think we should forget all this stuff about what might or might not be and just do our job."

And with that Ben got into Clarissa's cab. He'd already picked up their next assignment from the office and the red light on the notice board had just changed to green. Justin was at that moment solidifying out of the ether and into the passenger seat.

"Ready then?" asked Ben.

"Absolutely," replied Justin.

Clarissa lifted gently into the ether and glided through the veil into the sparkling blue sky of a summer's day down on Earth. This was what she loved. And she was happy.

She had found the driver who could tame her.

CHAPTER 17

The Challenge

Justin said he was off to the Lodge of Rest and Recuperation – visiting. Ben smiled. He knew who would be receiving Justin's care and attention at the hospital. *Young love. What a blessing it is.*

Their latest rescue case had been an easy one, quick and straightforward. Justin had included it in his notes though, another of his case studies.

"You know, I think that driver was very clued in to what had happened," remarked Justin. "Don't you?"

Ben stroked his chin. "Well, he certainly seemed to be waiting for us. Odd that. Haven't come across someone that ready before, except perhaps for Chrissie!" Justin grinned, remembering.

"This guy was really good to talk to,' Justin continued. "We had a great conversation about what he might expect of his new life, seemed to know something about it. What I could tell him wasn't that new to him, if you get my drift."

"Well, it certainly made our job much easier. He'll probably be in and out of the hospital before you can blink. Wonder what he'll do next? Did he say what he'd been before?"

"He used to work down a mine."

Ben caught himself almost being surprised, though why he should, he didn't know - he wasn't snobbish about such things. Why shouldn't a miner be clued up on the Summerland? "So he did a lot of reading? Spiritual books?"

"Not especially," Justin confirmed. "But his old Mum was psychic. A fatalist too, he said. Was always seeing things before they happened and believed there was a plan for everyone. So when he passed he sort of believed that was his plan and that he should just accept it. Said he'd seen his Mum clear as day, just before the car hit the barrier and tumbled over the edge into the valley. Made all the difference."

"So, a forewarning?"

"Yes. He said it was true that when the inevitable moment comes time slows down. It seemed to him he had hours to think through what was going on, see his Mum and talk to her, even saw his guardian and had a chat with him. All before the final crunch."

Ben winced momentarily at that word. But the feeling passed. "Nothing surprises me any more," he replied. "Every rescue I've been on so far has a different story to tell. And it all ends happily."

"There's someone here waiting for you, Ben."

Denis was rushing out of his office with a sheaf of papers and a spanner in his hand.

"Who, Denis?"

Too late, Denis had gone.

A man was standing with his back to the door, looking at the map on the opposite wall. It gave an up-to-date overview of the happenings at Station One Two Zero. Every now and again something changed on the map. Small images of ambulances disappeared or reappeared as they were taking off or returning to base; similarly, dot-like figures walked from one area to another, disappearing and reappearing.

"Fascinating," said the man turning around as Ben entered Denis's office.

"Doug! Well, I'll be blowed," said Ben. "What on Earth are you doing here?"

Doug had his usual lopsided grin and shook Ben's hand warmly. He'd been the station superintendent when they were both in the ambulance service in Bromley. Then Doug had retired and they'd lost contact. As you do.

"I heard you'd arrived a while ago, but didn't want to sidetrack you when you were obviously so busy."

"Yeah," Ben smiled, "they don't lose any time getting you a job here, do they?"

"You're recovered from the cancer op though?"

"You heard about that, too?"

"Well I asked. You know me, always like the details."

Ben could remember Doug's meticulous way of working, how every day on his shift he would check and double-check that the ambulances were in good working order, as well as the men! Wouldn't tolerate slackness, regardless of whether you had a good excuse or not. Thumping headaches could be dealt with, but if you arrived with a cold or, worse, `flu, he quickly sent you packing and off home no matter how keen you were to do your shift. "Our patients have enough to tolerate without you giving them your germs," he'd say.

He was a hard worker, was Doug, always early for his shift and last to go home. He seemed to be married to the job, some said, though he had a lovely wife and they had a very good relationship; but he and Gwen had never had children. He loved them though. If ever a job came in that took the ambulance crew to a children's ward, Doug would, if time allowed, go with them. And if a child was involved in an accident he wanted to know every detail of how they fared and what was being done for them. He would have made a loving father, but Ben realised that sometimes life doesn't always give us what we want; sometimes it takes us down an uneven path where the unexpected can compensate in odd ways. Ben used to think that Doug acted like a father to the young `uns, as he called the new recruits, whether they liked it or not. They came in fresh out of school, full of enthusiasm. Some would eventually have preferences: accidents and emergencies, or taking day patients to and from hospital. But all ambulance work had its rewards.

"They were good days," Doug said, coming out of a personal reverie, his eyes misting over. "God, I missed the job when I retired up north."

"What did you do with yourself then?"

"Lasted only two weeks up there. Had a stroke and then another in quick succession. Never had a chance, really. And poor Gwen, left in a place where she knew no-one."

"What did she do?"

"Moved back down south. She still had relatives there and she found a nice little bungalow near the south coast."

"Still over there then."

"Yep, she's still keeping going. I think she must be nearly eighty now. How time flies, it seems only yesterday since I arrived here."

"I know what you mean. I've not a clue how long I've been here. Not that I'm counting the days. Well, you can't really. Seems like one whole day, but different in that you never get tired. Time just seems to come and go without any sense of one day ending and another beginning, and it's so easy to get used to it. Barmy, isn't it?"

"Well, you might say that, but I think it's the only way to be. No clocks, no worry about ever being late for anything. And this telepathy thing, well, it's just the best, and no-one ever has a need to worry where you are 'cause they can just tune in to you. I call that perfect."

Ben grinned. Doug was right. It was all so different from how he remembered his previous Earthly existence. Doing shift work you had to constantly remind yourself what day of the week it was and the time of day, whether you were due to get up at dawn to do the early shift, or 10 o'clock at night to do the late one. The 3-11 p.m. was his favourite: a good lie-in in the morning was always a blessing. The night shift was the worst for those with young families, particularly pre-schoolers. Often wives had to take off for the day with the kids just so the man could get some peace and quiet, though that was difficult enough sometimes no matter how quiet the house was. Sleep didn't always come easy after a busy and difficult night; the adrenalin would still be pumping. In a way, Ben was glad to have left all that behind. He breathed a sigh of relief that all Earthly constraints simply didn't exist here.

"I've had to get used to this knowing there's time for everything, knowing there's no need to panic because you're never going to run out of it. Mind you, when we get an alert at the station then we're all hustle and bustle and can't get the chocks away quick enough."

"Did you spend much time at the hospital?" asked Doug.

"In recovery? Oh, yes. In fact I'd love to be there still, but you aren't encouraged to hang about. I have to say my expectations were seriously undermined at that point. I thought at least I'd be entitled to a little leisure time before being hauled straight back to work. This business of giving you a job as soon as you're well enough is a bit unfair, dishing out jobs when I was thinking how nice it would be to sit around doing absolutely nothing, even just for a short while. I haven't even had a holiday!"

Doug laughed out loud. "You wouldn't have liked it, Ben. You'd have been bored stiff within a micro-blink of an eye."

"Well, I'll never know because I wasn't given the chance even to consider it."

Doug laughed again. "I bet you love the life."

Ben nodded. It was true, he did.

"I've come to see you, old friend," said Doug, "because I heard you were asking about the medical school at the university."

"You've been talking to Brian."

"Have you some free time to talk?"

"I'd better check with Denis first."

"It all looks taken care of, as far as I can see," said Doug as he glanced over Ben's shoulder at the missions board. "How about we find a quiet spot where we can talk?"

They relocated to a part of the Gardens of Remembrance Ben hadn't visited before. They were sitting on a garden bench that had conveniently materialised in front of them, in the midst of a small grove of trees, when a small furry figure began to coalesce out of the ether. Rufus.

"He yours?" asked Doug.

"Yes. He likes to visit. He used to be quite scruffy, but I've found out that not only is he handsome, he's also quite chatty."

Doug laughed. "Yes, that's one thing that took me by surprise when I first came here. The ability to actually converse with animals is quite a shock."

"Well, Rufus came at a time when I needed to remember how it was to be loved - and that we should never feel alone."

Doug bent down to stroke Rufus. "Good dog." Rufus took the hint and lay down, closing his eyes.

"Did you work at the ambulance station when *you* first arrived?" asked Ben.

"Yes, enjoyed it immensely. It's a great and wonderful job, helping people when they can't find their way home on their own."

"But you've moved on to bigger things?"

"Not bigger, just different. I never thought I would be any good at studying. But I've been doing it for a while now. It's an amazing thing to find out you can be a bit of an academic." Doug was being modest, Ben could tell. "Didn't know much about anything before, other than ambulance work," Doug added, "but the university here caters for all sorts, even beginners. There are schools for every subject you can think of. Anyway, I took the plunge and enrolled in the Medical School. It's run by a team of professors who are all experts in their field, and then there are the smaller sprats like me who have got enough under our belt to start tutoring the first year students." Ben could tell Doug was being modest again. "Like you, when I left the hospital my first thought was to spend some time getting to know my way around, see the place, but ... "

"They didn't even give you the time to consider it."

"Well, it wasn't quite like that. I just found I had an irresistible urge to do something useful. I went back to the hospital, wanting to help out. Quite a lot of former patients do that. The end result was that it inspired me to want to go on to further study."

"What's it like, this Medical School?"

"Just like any conventional such place in a lot of ways - a large building, several departments, labs."

"I hear the university is quite big."

"Big doesn't even begin to describe it. Everything and anything you want to learn is there. You see, most professions that exist on Earth have their counterpart here. Or you could say that in reverse and it would still be true."

"So these medical students, how do they make up their minds that this is what they want to do? Is it an idea they bring over with them, like an ambition never fulfilled?"

"Some of them have had prior experience in the medical profession and find they want to branch out into another speciality, still in the medical line but something they didn't have the chance to do before. And others are complete newcomers to anything medical."

Ben was intrigued and wanted to know more. "So, when they reincarnate back on Earth, do any of these new skills get remembered?"

"Yes, quite often, but then there's always free will. Someone might have an aptitude for something but decide not to follow it through. It's always a personal choice, even if they regret it later. But then I've been told there's no such thing as a mistake. All our choices are made out of the gift of free will. It's how we learn."

"And some, like me," added Ben, "like to do things the hard way – make lots of mistakes."

"Well, you wouldn't be alone. When you meet the students you'll find there are all sorts. What people once did in their former life is no reflection of what they might be interested in doing now, or what choices they might make."

Ben was thinking that he hadn't exactly experienced that so far, though there was no doubt that he'd ended up in the right place. But this university thing was beginning to sound good, something even *he* could take on and perhaps not such a big challenge after all.

It was time for Doug to go. They shook hands again, promising to keep in touch. "Probably see you at the university, if not at the hospital."

As Doug's energy melted back into the ether, allowing thought to take him to his next port of call, the realisation suddenly came to Ben that somehow someone had known how much he had needed this chat with an old friend. It had helped him make up his mind.

There was just another little passing thought, enough for Ben to voice to the ether in case anyone was listening: *I hope you guys aren't planning too much ahead, especially when I might want to think about some things for a while longer.*

Rufus looked up at his master, suddenly awake and ears pricked in an unspoken signal. Ben bent down to stroke him. "I'm needed back at base am I?"

"Woof!"

165

Together they crossed the large expanse of lawn that led down a gentle incline towards a gateway. Beyond lay all the paths that led in and out of the gardens. They took the one signposted *Fulfilment*. Ben realised it was what he wanted most of all.

At Station One Two Zero, he put a tick against his name on the message board outside the station office to indicate he was available and on standby. Denis looked at him enquiringly, sensing a subtle change.

"Had some good news then?"

Ben smiled and nodded. "Yep, and I think the next time you find my paperwork for the university you'd better hang on to it. I might be ready to sign on."

Denis gripped the desk to keep himself from falling over. "Right you are. I'm on to it. Don't go away!"

Ben looked down at his beloved dog. "Well, old chum, I have to get to work," and pointed to the other message board, which relayed missions waiting to be fulfilled.

"Ok," woofed Rufus, still in thought-mode. "Shall I pop by again?" He cocked his head on one side, waiting for Ben to make the choice.

"Of course," said Ben, smiling. "Come by anytime I'm free. I'm sure you'll know when that is. Everyone here seems to know the right time for everything." He waited for Rufus to turn away, watching him for a millisecond before he disappeared into the ether, off to do whatever little dogs did.

Clarissa was warmed up and ready to leave. Ben ran his hand gently along her bonnet as he moved to open the driver's door. Clarissa's senses were on immediate alert as she cast a sideways glance.

"What is it, Ben?"

"I don't really know. I just feel that everything is about to change, but I'm not sure I'm ready for it."

"Your epaulettes haven't changed colour yet, have they?" she asked anxiously.

"No, Claris, not yet, not for a long time yet. Don't worry." He patted her bonnet to reassure her. He knew she wasn't looking forward to the day his epaulettes did change, though he couldn't imagine they ever would. And why would they? He was quite happy doing what he was doing, rescuing people, working with his special ambulance.

"So, this feeling you have, it can't be about you going off to do something else then, something different?" she asked.

"It might just be to do with me going to the university. And you know how I feel about that!"

"All I know is that it's inevitable. Everyone has to be educated sometime or other. Some take ages before they make up their mind. I'm sure the choice is up to you." Clarissa sounded hopeful.

Ben smiled, a wry grin rather. "I have a feeling that I'm being urged, rather than given a choice."

"Yes, well, I know you've got to do it, but there's no reason to think you won't still have a job here. Is there?"

"I guess not."

"Well, then, stop grumping and go get our co-ordinates from Denis."

"Yes, madam, anything you say."

Denis met him half-way. "There you go, lad. Look sharp. A mishap in the Scottish Isles. Outer Hebrides."

Ben settled into the cushioned comfort of his seat and buckled up, just as Justin appeared in the seat beside him.

"Ok, Claris," said Ben, letting out the brake pads, "let's see who we can bring safely home."

And with that Clarissa winged her way up and away, humming a little tune she'd just made up, skimming etheric currents and the occasional cloud on the way.

Printed in August 2023
by Rotomail Italia S.p.A., Vignate (MI) - Italy